Civil War Ghosts

SWEETWATER
PRESS

Civil War Ghosts
Copyright © 2006 by Sweetwater Press
Produced by Cliff Road Books

ISBN-13: 978-1-58173-540-6
ISBN-10: 1-58173-540-5

Book design by Pat Covert

Printed in the United States of America

Civil War Ghosts

they are among us

Brice Camp

SWEETWATER
PRESS

Table of Contents

They Are Among Us

They Are Among Us

It seems only natural that war, which results in the death and suffering of so many, would also result in legends and myths. Among these, one can always find a good ghost story or two, but this is especially the case with the Civil War. The legacy of the Civil War is positively rife with stories of spirits and haints who linger in the world of the living.

These ghost stories enjoy such a robust life partly due to the centralization of the war in the South. Most of the action of the war occurred in the Southeast, a region which places a high premium on a good story or tall tale. Though ghosts and spooks pervade all locales the Civil War touched, they really seem to be out and about in droves in the South, which can't get enough of its ghosts and legends.

But it's not only heroes and soldiers and generals and drummer boys that are represented, for the war impacted civilians too. Slaves, wives, children, sweethearts—nobody was left unmoved by the bloody conflict that lasted a mere four years. These four years shaped collective memory both national and regional, forging the identities of Americans both Northern and

Southern, creating some of our nation's brief history's greatest heroes.

Maybe the permanent impression this war made on Americans is what prompts us to latch on to the ghost stories. Maybe these ghosts and spirits are just a metaphor for the lingering influence of the great American war, the war that pitted region versus region, but also brother against brother. So passionate and personal was this war that even a century of time cannot erase the impact. Maybe these ghosts represent the memory of a time in our nation's history that refuses to be forgotten.

But maybe, just maybe, these phantoms and apparitions are more than just a metaphorical creation. Is the war chant of the Irish Brigade still echoing across the hills of Antietam? Is the weeping nurse still tending to the dying and wounded in an old plantation home in Mississippi? Is a Union general still standing bravely alongside his men in a grove in Stones River? Does John Brown still wander the streets of Harper's Ferry where he made his audacious raid? Does Old Green Eyes still inhabit the woods at Chickamauga? Some readers may think it's all ridiculous, but don't dare say so to those who purport to have seen these paranormal beings. Some readers may believe it, having had a supernatural experience themselves. Most readers, however, will probably feel a little bit of both. By reading this little collection of stories, maybe they'll be inspired to visit these important places and find out for themselves.

It should be noted that ghost stories are one of the few lingering vestiges of our oral tradition. As such, they tend to grow and change with time, sometimes embellished to give a story a little kick. Names and other details are often changed to protect those who've witnessed unbelievable sights. The Civil War ghost stories are no exception, and they grow creepier and more interesting with every retelling. Just because a teller may be guilty of a little exaggeration does not mean these tales should be wholly dismissed. Maybe you'll retell some of these stories yourself and add a few details for good measure, just as long as you keep the stories alive.

So, take these tales with a grain of salt and an open mind, if you can do both at once. Read, consider, and see what you think, but above all, enjoy these stories. And if you like them, don't worry. There's plenty more where these came from.

Brice Camp

Faugh-a-Balaugh

Faugh-a-Balaugh

The boisterous group of school kids clambered excitedly onto the school bus, laughing and jostling each other noisily as they took their seats. They were on their way to historic Antietam Battlefield, but this mattered little to them. All they knew was a field trip was definitely better than a day stuck in school.

The school kids had grown up in Maryland close enough to Antietam Battlefield to know something about it, but their teacher hoped that a field trip to the actual site in Sharpsburg, Maryland, might help them understand the battle and the Civil War in a way a history book could not.

Before the field trip, the students had learned about the particulars. They knew that in September of 1862, over the course of a single day, more Union and Confederate soldiers were killed or wounded than on any other day of the War—10,700 Confederate soldiers and 12,410 Union soldiers, to be exact. Although the numbers are staggering, they seemed to be just that to the students—numbers. The reality of such death and devastation was lost on them.

The bunch was lively and excited on the way to

the battlefield, relieved to be free from desks and lectures for an entire day. They arrived at the battlefield and looked around expectantly, only to be disappointed by their seemingly ordinary surroundings. They weren't sure what they were expecting, but vacant, grassy fields like the ones around their own houses were definitely not it.

They met their tour guide, Ethan Miller, a youthfully exuberant man despite his many years. He was obviously fascinated by the Civil War and Antietam in particular, and immediately began to try to pique their interest. His excitement was tempered with reverence, but the fervor with which he regarded the battlefield was tangible, and as he led them around the hallowed ground his enthusiasm became infectious.

Through vivid descriptions Ethan managed to inspire the kids' imaginations, helping them to visualize the horrific events that occurred right where they were standing. It gave them a chill to think that so much death and destruction had occurred in such a deceptively tranquil place.

Ethan finally led them to the Sunken Road, a location in the battle so devastating that it earned the moniker "Bloody Lane." This colorful but morbid name caught the kids' attention, and they stood riveted as the guide walked them down the old country road.

"As far as we know, this lane looks just the way it did on September 17 over a hundred years ago, with one exception," he explained. He gestured to the furrowed dirt road beneath the children's feet and said quietly, "You could have walked the entire length of this road and never touched the ground. There were so many dead men piled on this road that in some places they were three bodies deep."

Ethan paused and let this sink in. The kids were wide-eyed with awe and horror, instinctively looking under and around them as if they might see the mangled body of a Confederate soldier reaching for their ankle. The air seemed to grow a bit colder and the students were deathly silent.

The guide gestured expansively toward a small hill that sloped down to meet the Sunken Road. He explained that when the two Confederate brigades first held the road, it was a terrific advantage. They were ordered to hold the road at all costs, and hold it they did. The Union soldiers would appear on the horizon of the little hill only to be swiftly cut down by the Confederates lying in wait on the lane.

Among the Union forces decimated by the onslaught of Rebel fire was the 69th of New York, also known as the Irish Brigade. Ethan looked over the sea of hushed and expectant faces and said gravely, "More than sixty percent of the Irish Brigade was slaughtered that day. Look around you. Look at your classmates. There are maybe thirty of you. What if eighteen of you didn't make it home?"

"This guy is good," the teacher thought approvingly, standing behind her class, quite pleased with the tour so far. She could already see that the tour was having an impact on her students, helping them to understand the grisly and horrific nature of the battle in a way she never could in a classroom.

"But they just kept swarming over the hill, falling to the ground dead nearly as soon as they crested the peak. Some of them weren't much older than you." Ethan mentioned this last part casually, almost as an afterthought, but its desired effect was achieved. The students gazed at the hill beyond their guide, shivering to imagine the waves of young soldiers collapsing on the bloody grass.

Ethan explained that the Confederate advantage didn't outlast the battle, however. The Union troops were able to flank the brigades on the Sunken Road, gaining a high ground that allowed them to fire on the Rebels.

"After that, this road really earned its name, 'Bloody Lane,'" he told them somberly. "Once the Union soldiers had the high ground it was like

15

shooting fish in a barrel. It was a slaughter," he said dolefully, "an absolute slaughter."

"Imagine the noise: cannons thumping in the distance, the deafening clap of musket fire all around you, the sound of agony and screams. Imagine the fear: you're lying here on a road," Ethan said, lying on the ground for effect, "there are hundreds of guys above you shooting your friends and comrades, and you're frantically trying to load your musket to defend yourself." He fumbled with imaginary weaponry and looked up to where the Union soldiers had been with theatrical fear.

"There's blood everywhere, body parts everywhere, and you're struggling to stay alive, knowing that at any moment a Union bullet might catch you between the eyes. You might even happen to look up in time to see the soldier who shot that fatal bullet. If you were lucky maybe you'd just lose your arms, or your legs…or both. Just imagine for a moment what that might have been like."

Here he paused and the kids did just that—they tried to imagine such an awful scenario, exchanging sidelong glances with friends in intense and wordless communication. The tour had started out interesting enough, but this was starting to really get to them.

Sensing that he had fully impressed Bloody Lane

upon the students, Ethan broke the spell and spirited them along to Burnside Bridge, another site in the tragic battle. After showing them the Bridge and other points of interest, he ended the tour with a cryptic remark: "As you walk around the battleground today, never forget that this is hallowed ground. Thousands of people just like you and me perished here, and some say, linger still."

As he walked away from the entranced students Ethan smiled a bit to himself at this last piece of theatricality. Antietam, like most Civil War battlefields, was alleged to be haunted by specters and spirits. He was grateful for the curiosity it inspired and the added business it drummed up for the park, but he himself thought the reality of the actual event interesting enough to merit a visit. The seasoned guide discounted whatever rumors and stories he had heard about his beloved battlefield, taking some of the responsibility for encouraging people's overactive imaginations.

The students stood in respectful silence as the guide turned and walked away. Their teacher quietly directed them to wander about the grounds at will, being careful to make notes about how the experience made them feel.

A group of boys, still transfixed by the horrific descriptions of Bloody Lane, took off immediately for the notorious road. The afternoon was growing dimmer and their shadows were long in front of them. They tried to keep the mood light by horsing around, pretending to be Confederate soldiers, brandishing guns, marching in step.

When they got to the spot in the road where the guide had explained the tragic events to them, however, they grew more somber. They separated but made sure to keep each other in sight.

One of the boys, Mark, stood with his chin on the split rail fence that lined the road, gazing up at the hill where members of the Irish Brigade once charged bravely to their deaths. His imagination ran so wild that he had to blink to be sure he didn't see their ghosts struggling over the summit.

Mark could hear his fellow classmates chanting and singing something just up the road, no doubt trying to reenact some of the horrors relayed to them by the guide, and he turned peevishly toward the sound. He had been very moved by what he had seen that day and was a little irritated that his classmates weren't taking it as seriously as he was. His mood completely spoiled, he begrudgingly set off in the direction of the chanting to walk back to the bus with his friends, but the sound seemed to fade as he approached them.

When he caught up with them, Mark asked them what they had been singing. It sounded familiar.

His friends swore up and down that they hadn't been chanting; they thought he was the one getting carried away and making all the racket. They shrugged it off as another tour group somewhere in the park and took off for the bus and the rest of their class.

When they got back to the bus Ethan awaited them to say goodbye. As the students filed onto the bus, he asked them if they saw anything interesting.

"Well, we didn't see anything but we heard something kinda weird," one boy said. "We walked back up to Bloody Lane and it sounded like someone was singing, 'Deck the Halls' or something like that. We all heard it but couldn't figure out where it was coming from. That's kinda weird. It's not even Christmas. I guess it was another tour group or something."

The boy didn't notice but Ethan furrowed his brow and eyed him closely. "'Deck the Halls,' huh?" he tried to ask casually, knowing full well that the school group would be the last to leave the park.

"Yeah, you know, 'Fa-la-la-la-la-la-la-la-la,'" the boy sang tunelessly.

Ethan smiled absently and nodded before saying goodbye abruptly and turning to leave. It was the end of the day and time to go home, but his feet directed him back toward Bloody Lane.

As the wind blew across the grass and the sun dipped lower behind the trees, the guide cocked his head and listened closely. He tuned his ears and stood for several minutes, waiting to hear something.

But what he was waiting to hear was not the refrain of "Deck the Halls." Although he had always been a skeptic about ghosts, he reluctantly admitted to himself that if there were ever a place where tortured souls might linger, Bloody Lane was it. He knew deep down that what the boys had heard was not a Christmas carol at all.

As Ethan stood silently in the Sunken Road, the words, "Faugh-a-Balaugh! Faugh-a-Balaugh!" echoed in his head. He knew the Irish Brigade had charged into a hail of bullets yelling this very battle cry, a Gaelic phrase meaning "Clear the Way!" His breath grew shallower as the battle cry seemed to grow louder and louder in his ears. It rolled up and over the hill with a hollow, reverberated sound, peppered with the rumble of cannon fire and the sharp crack of muskets. He could practically see the members of the Irish Brigade screaming in their native tongue as they fell to the ground that bloody day. The image became so vivid and the sound so clear in his mind that the guide's

20

hands flew to his ears as he shut his eyes tightly and shook his head.

He was certain beyond a shadow of a doubt that the boys could not have known that such a cry was uttered there, nor did he suspect they could have all mistakenly heard the same song, let alone in an empty park. He began to wonder…

The old guide finally opened his eyes and exhaled loudly. "You're getting soft, old man," he thought to himself. If he wasn't careful, pretty soon he would start believing every absurd ghost story that came his way.

He had walked this road countless times in his tenure as a tour guide at Antietam. But, that day, as he headed back for the land of the living, he walked a little quicker than usual, trying to escape the sounds of the Ghost Brigade crying "Faugh-a-Balaugh! Faugh-a-Balaugh!"

The Ghost with the Wounded Leg

The Ghost with the Wounded Leg

A "fixer-upper" Michael called it. Carol took a good bit of convincing before she agreed to move into the old antebellum home about halfway between Corinth and Shiloh. He said it had more character than you could shake a stick at, but the absurdly narrow stairways, warped old-fashioned glass windows and sloping floors did little to interest the young woman. She had wanted something modern and spacious, but her newlywed bliss had not yet worn off and she didn't want to disappoint him. Always a history buff, he just seemed so excited about the prospect of living in a two hundred-year-old house, she couldn't bring herself to say no.

Carol had heard that it had been used as a hospital at some point, which wasn't surprising to her husband. He explained to her that Shiloh had been a major battle between 65,000 Union troops and 44,000 Confederate troops. She guessed that was a lot. A few miles southwest down the road was Corinth, Mississippi, where the Union soldiers seized control of the Confederate railroad system. Her husband got wide-eyed and excited just talking about this stuff, but

24

she couldn't care less. She had her hands so full with a new baby that she just wanted to get moved in and settled.

All of their worldly possessions were still in boxes. The mountains of boxes looked daunting, but Carol knew that even after it was all unpacked they would still have a hard time filling up the huge house. Not exactly a typical starter home, this house. She was sure that once they got settled she would get used to all the space.

While the baby was taking a nap upstairs, Carol started shuffling through some of the boxes. She picked up a heavy box intended for the kitchen that the movers had accidentally brought upstairs. She was about to head downstairs when she noticed a strange stain on the floor. She put the box down and stooped to look at it. It was a large dark stain with a few smaller ones next to it. She assumed that a house that old was bound to a have a few stains and shrugged it off.

Carol heard the baby wake up from her nap and ran in to check on her. She held Mary who usually stopped crying after a few laps around the room, but she hadn't adjusted well to the new surroundings. She was extremely fussy lately, which was out of character for her.

The young mother carried her tiny baby down to the kitchen where she got a bottle out of the refrigerator. The refrigerator looked oddly out of place in the antique kitchen, but she was glad the previous owners had left it. They had left a lot of stuff actually, because they had to move out quickly for some reason or another. That was probably why they were able to get the huge, old house for so cheap.

While she gave the bottle to Mary, she wandered out onto the porch. A big rambling porch wrapped around the entire house, which was one of the few things she actually liked about it. As she strolled slowly with the baby, she noticed another stain on the porch. It was a ring of the same color as the ones she had seen upstairs.

She added "paint for the porch" onto her steadily growing list of things that needed to be done to get her new home into shape. She got tired just thinking about all the work that needed to be done.

When Michael got home from work she showed him the weird stains she had discovered. She was surprised that he was thrilled by the discovery.

"I've seen stains like this in old houses before. Remember how we heard this place was used as a makeshift hospital during the war? It's probably blood! How cool is that!"

"Not very," the young wife said dryly. "Call me crazy, but I thought bloodstains were something you wanted to avoid having on the floor."

"It's history, honey! How many houses can say they have bloodstains from a battle over a hundred years ago?! I bet the one on the porch was a bucket of blood!" He was ecstatic. She was far from it.

That night Carol had trouble sleeping. While Michael snored softly next to her she listened to the "house settling" noises that are so much louder in a house that old. "House settling," he called it. She called it annoying. She was having trouble sleeping in this house, but she told herself she just wasn't used to it yet. It felt so cold and empty compared to their cozy little apartment they had left behind. She'd learn to love it, she thought, and satisfied with this thought though still a little dubious, she rolled over and went to sleep.

The next day Michael had to leave town on business. She wasn't crazy about being in that big house all alone, certainly not at night, but she was glad he was doing so well. It was a relief to know that he could support them until the baby was old enough and she could go back to work.

"I'll be back tomorrow around three. Here's the number of the hotel they put me in. Call me if you need anything. I love you."

"I love you too," she said and hugged him tightly. As she stood on the blood stained porch and watched him drive away, she found herself not wanting to go back inside. She had never bought a house before, but she supposed that that wasn't the way she should feel buying her first house.

Eager to "get used to it" as her husband kept telling her she would, she began unpacking and cleaning with renewed fervor. By late afternoon the place did start to feel a little cozier. A few paintings on the walls and furniture arranged to give the rooms some semblance of roominess made a big difference. As she hung a painting her friend had made over a fireplace, she felt relieved to see something familiar in the house. It started to feel a little more like her own.

As Carol worked on the house, however, she got a little freaked out from time to time. The thought that so much death and pain had occurred right here in her house made her uncomfortable. While it made her husband ecstatic that so much history had occurred in their house, she couldn't help but feel that all that suffering had left behind bad vibes. She wasn't overly superstitious, but she didn't rule out that sometimes weird stuff happens that can't be explained.

Whenever her imagination would turn toward

amputated limbs and buckets of blood she would force herself to think of something else. Unfortunately, trying not to think of something is fundamentally impossible for most people, and she was one of them. She wondered how long it would take for her to get really comfortable here.

After the sun went down she turned on every light in the house and the television. The noise made her feel a little better. Luckily, between unpacking and taking care of her daughter, she had plenty of distractions. She got a few phone calls from friends checking in on her which brightened her spirits. After she put Mary to bed, however, she had to be extra quiet. As fussy as the baby had been lately, she couldn't risk waking her. It would be another two hours before she got her to sleep again.

A few hours later Carol tiptoed up to Mary's room at the end of the hall upstairs, opened and shut the door quietly and crept over to the crib to check on her. She was sleeping peacefully, for which the young mother was grateful. She was about to tiptoe back out of the room when she heard something strange.

"Were those footsteps?" she thought to herself. She froze and cocked her head to listen.

"Oh my gosh, those are definitely footsteps. Is Michael home early? No, he would have called if he were coming home early," she thought with growing hysteria.

The footsteps were definitely approaching the door. It sounded like a step and a drag, a step and a drag, a step and a drag, like someone with an injured leg.

Carol was literally shaking with fear and panic. The steps moved deliberately closer. Her heart was thumping deafeningly in her ears and her breathing was shallow and quick. In a cold sweat, she looked around the baby's room for something to defend herself and her baby. Cursing herself for not having unpacked the baby's things earlier, she tried to keep her hysterical tears as silent as possible. Her eyes finally fell on an iron poker that hung by the fireplace. She grabbed it and stood in front of the crib, brandishing it like a sword but shaking violently.

The intruder stepped and dragged closer and closer. The steps finally stopped just outside the door. She wanted desperately to close her eyes but knew she had to be ready for whoever was coming. She stifled a scream with her hand and waited, trembling.

When the door flew open there was no one there. Somehow that was worse than an actual person standing there.

Michael was awakened by frantic banging on his hotel room door. He was sluggish from still being half-asleep but jumped up and ran to the door. He looked through the peephole and saw his wife and baby. In a panic, he flung the door open.

Carol tumbled into the room in tears, babbling incoherently. Michael grabbed Mary and laid her on the bed and took his wife by the shoulders. He shook her gently to get her to focus enough to tell him what was going on.

"We're selling the house. I love you honey, but I will never set foot in that house ever, ever again," she said firmly. She found that she could barely relate to him what had happened without getting upset all over again.

The young couple stayed in the hotel for the next few days. They moved out and put the house on the market the next week. Michael tried gently to convince Carol that she had been dreaming, that it was just her imagination, that they should give the house another chance. The young woman knew what she had seen and did not appreciate being told she just thought she had seen it. For the sake of the marriage and her sanity, Michael finally agreed to move out. Now he understood why the house was so cheap and why it was the previous owners abandoned it so quickly.

Years later Michael was driving to Shiloh on business and decided to swing by and take a look at

31

the house that had been his for a grand total of four days. But when he pulled onto the road, he was shocked to see that the house was gone. There was no trace of the old antebellum plantation home or of the auxiliary houses that had been positioned behind it. Apparently someone had apparently taken it upon themselves to exorcise the demons. After all, who wanted to live in a haunted house?

Slaughter Pen

Slaughter Pen

Dan Brooks, the Stones River groundskeeper, checked his watch and was pleased to see that it was almost five o'clock. He felt like he had been over every square inch of the six-hundred-acre battlefield about a hundred times that day. The intense summer sun of Tennessee had sucked out whatever energy he had left after the physical labor was done with him. He could have retired a few years ago, but every year he found himself saying, "One more year, one more year." One of these days, though...

The heat had kept sightseers and Civil War buffs to a minimum, allowing Dan to putter around with his thoughts. He knew the park like the back of his hand, having tended to it lovingly for years. However, his long tenure had whittled away the mystique and excitement of its historical significance, so his imagination had long since stopped turning to the brutal and bloody events that had transpired at the battlefield.

Dan used to picture the battle that occurred at Stones River all the time. His imagination would conjure up images of General Bragg's Confederate

soldiers surprising the Union soldiers commanded by
General Rosencrans, leaving only one Union division
ready to fight. He would imagine the gory details of
the bloody battle, a battle that claimed the lives of
roughly a third of both sides of the conflict. He would
get especially fired up when he worked around what
was known as "The Slaughter Pen," a cedar grove on
the battlefield where fighting was especially fierce—
hence the colorful but morbid name.

The one alert division, led by General Sheridan,
had taken its position in the small grove of trees,
trying desperately to hold the Confederates back while
the other divisions scrambled to organize. They held
out until their ammunition ran out, at which point
they resorted to rocks, fists, bayonets, and whatever
else they could find to stave off the Confederate
onslaught. Needless to say, this area saw a lot of blood,
gore, and death, and the groundskeeper used to
picture it all in his mind.

After a while, however, Dan began to see the
Slaughter Pen as he saw the rest of the park, as a
historically significant place that demanded respect,
but also demanded physical labor to ensure its upkeep
and his paycheck. He had heard all the rumors about
ghosts and ghouls supposedly hanging out in the
Slaughter Pen, but he chalked the stories up to the

enthusiastic imaginings of overzealous Civil War buffs. According to him, they saw all of that paranormal hogwash because they wanted to see it so badly. With a little creativity and imagination, a person could convince himself that he had seen just about anything.

On that hot summer day Dan was feeling especially pragmatic, ready to finish up his work so he could go home and take a cold shower. He thought to himself that he wouldn't have minded being on this battlefield for the actual fighting, because at least on New Year's Eve in 1862 it wouldn't have been this dang hot. Then he reminded himself of the brutal and bloody details of the gory battle and decided he'd rather grapple with the sun.

Dan wandered over to the Slaughter Pen to retrieve some of his equipment he had left in the shade. As he stooped over to pick up his tools he groaned a little. Maybe it was time to throw in the towel and retire; he was getting too old for this job. At least it was relatively cooler in the shade of the cedars.

As he straightened back up he heard the crunch of footsteps behind him. He had been left in quiet solitude so long that the sound made him jump. He was so startled he dropped what he had just gone to all the trouble to pick up in the first place. He turned around quickly but didn't see anything. "Must've been a squirrel," he thought and stooped over to pick up his equipment, groaning a little louder this time.

A cool breeze blew through the trees as he righted himself. All of a sudden he had that strange feeling like he knew he was being watched. He scanned the trees around him, but saw nothing but the same old trees he'd been looking at for years.

Dan was just getting ready to go store his equipment when he heard it again, the crunch of footsteps behind him. This time when he turned around he did see something—a man with a dark moustache walking through the trees. Another one of those re-enactors, it looked like.

"Hey there, park's about to close up for the day. Might wanna start heading back to your car."

The mustachioed man said nothing, looking around with an intense look of concentration.

"You looking for something sir? Better hurry up and find it before we close up shop."

Again, the man said nothing, but continued striding toward the groundskeeper purposefully.

"Say, you look kinda familiar. Have we met? I must have seen you at a re-enactment or something." Dan's attempts at small talk were obviously falling on deaf ears. The strange man had his jaw set like he was concentrating fiercely, but what he was doing there was a mystery to the groundskeeper. He was, however, naggingly familiar. The groundskeeper knew the face from somewhere, he just couldn't place it.

"Well look, sir, the park's hours are eight to five. If you wanna come back tomorrow, you're more than welcome to," he said a little testily.

Again the man said nothing. "What a weirdo," Dan thought. He was a little irritable from the heat and fatigue, so he was losing patience. "Suit yourself, buddy. If you wanna sleep here, be my guest." He looked over his shoulder a few times at the mysterious park visitor, seeing the dark, intense man heading off into the woods in the opposite direction. With that he carried his equipment back to his truck and drove toward the main building that served as the Visitor's Center for the park. He would drop off his equipment, get a cold drink from the drink machine, tell whoever he could find about the weirdo out in the Slaughter Pen, hop in his truck, and head home to put his feet up. The idea sounded so good to him that he quickened his pace a bit.

Dan stored his equipment and was pleased to find the doors to the Visitor's Center still open. He walked inside and sighed contentedly at the wave of cool air that hit him. He realized he needed to make a little rest stop before he got in his car to go home, so he took off in the direction of the restrooms.

As he was walking he was thinking how nice it must be to work indoors sometimes. The cool, quiet center was quite comfortable to the groundskeeper who was still mopping sweat from his brow. Sometimes he would go all day without setting foot inside.

He had seen everything in the Visitor's Center a hundred times, but he felt compelled to take a look at some of the pictures hanging on the wall. The first photograph his eyes fell on made him stop abruptly. He felt a chill rush through his body as every hair on his body stood at attention. He could hear the blood rushing in his ears.

"Oh my gosh," he said quietly to himself. "It can't be. There's no way."

The picture he looked at was a portrait, much like any other portrait taken during the Civil War era. It was a portrait of General Phil Sheridan, the general who commanded the division that was obliterated in the Slaughter Pen.

Suddenly, Dan realized where he had seen that weirdo in the park earlier. He had seen him in this picture, a picture taken when he was still alive over a hundred years ago.

He shook his head in disbelief. As he gazed into the eyes of the man in the portrait, he knew beyond a shadow of a doubt that he had gazed into those eyes that day in the Slaughter Pen. He felt like the picture itself was looking at him and he was entranced, hypnotized by the face that he hadn't been able to place.

Abruptly he turned and took off for his car. As he started his car and backed out of the parking place, a thought crossed his mind briefly, "Maybe it is time to retire." He chuckled to himself, but he knew deep down that this time, he meant it.

The Ghost of John Brown

The Ghost of John Brown

This was exactly how they had planned to spend their retirement: cruising around the country in an RV, enjoying their golden years by taking in everything America had to offer. They had been to all of the lower forty-eight states many times over, but every time they went somewhere they managed to see something new and exciting.

Sometimes they just drove aimlessly, letting themselves be carried along by whimsy and chance. Other times there was an agenda, a theme for their trip. Last year they hit all the biggest roller coasters around the country. The year before that they did Route 66. This year, they decided, would be a Civil War tour.

Morris and Edna both knew a little bit about the war, but only what they could remember from high school history class, which was a lot longer ago than they cared to admit. As avid RVers, however, they knew that they could learn more in a couple of months on the road than they could in a semester's worth of history classes.

They had already been to Gettysburg, Antietam,

Richmond, and now they were headed to Harper's Ferry, West Virginia.

"What happened at Harper's Ferry again? I think I've heard of it before," Morris said, "I'm just too old to remember anything at all anymore."

Edna looked it up in one of the reference books she had brought along for just such a purpose. She told him that Harper's Ferry was synonymous with John Brown, a famous abolitionist.

"Listen to what this guy said: 'Here, before God, in the presence of these witnesses, I consecrate my life to the destruction of slavery,'" the woman read aloud from the book.

Edna explained to her husband that in 1859, this die-hard abolitionist had gathered up a small army and marched into Harper's Ferry, where he seized the armory, the arsenal, and the engine house. The purpose of this dramatic act was to arm the slaves of the area. He had brought with him pikes, guns, knives, and other weapons so that the slaves he wished to free might fight alongside him for their freedom.

It turned into a rather bloody ordeal, she read aloud, after hostages were taken by Brown and his gang. Then they fired upon a train. The people of Harper's Ferry were none too pleased by this, and took to the streets to do battle with the ardent abolitionist and his men.

The government sent troops from Washington to quell the raid that had by that point already caused the death of a free black man in the village. Interestingly enough, these troops were led by Robert E. Lee.

"Now even I can remember who he was," Morris said with a chuckle.

Edna went on to explain that the troops managed to breach the arsenal, wound John Brown, and put an end to the rebellious raid. Brown was put on trial for treason in Virginia a few months later.

"He was hanged on December 2 of that same year. Wow, the justice system sure moved a lot quicker then than it does now," Edna marveled. "This John Brown character was extremely brave but it also sounds like he may have been a little crazy."

"At least he stood up for what he believed in," Morris said.

They pulled into the small West Virginia town, parked the RV, and got out. It felt good to stretch their legs after sitting in the car for five hours. They were ready to start sightseeing, but first they needed something to eat. The town was a charming and beautiful one, and they enjoyed strolling around until they found a spot to eat.

After lunch they meandered around the village, trying to imagine what it would have looked like back on that fateful day in 1859. The book had done a good job of explaining exactly why that day was so important. It galvanized people on both sides of the slavery issue. It generated more support for the abolitionist movement on one hand, and infuriated those who thought it was reckless and treacherous behavior. Some even say that it was one of the major catalysts of the war itself.

They were disappointed to find out that only the armory, known now as "John Brown's fort" had survived the Civil War. They walked all around it taking pictures while the woman continued reading from her book.

"This is where the troops had to fight their way in to capture John Brown. What a dedicated man! It says here that two of his sons were killed in the raid," she read.

They got a fellow sightseer to snap a picture of them standing in front of the fort. They thanked the man, who told them that he had seen a John Brown look-a-like in town.

"He's a spitting image of the actual John Brown. I guess the park hires him as a history actor or something. Maybe because there isn't all that much to see, they needed to spice things up a bit. Anyhow, you should go take a look."

The couple thanked him for the tip and strolled

down the road to find him. Edna referenced the book that had an old portrait of Brown on one of the pages, and they started looking around for the supposed look-alike.

"There he is," Morris said, and they headed toward the man.

The other tourist had been right. As they approached, they could tell that he did indeed look just like the famous abolitionist. He had a headful of wiry hair, a big bushy beard, and a haggard face. They snapped a few pictures of him and waved. He didn't wave back but did give them a small smile as they strolled past.

"Maybe he's like one of those Buckingham Palace guards, y'know, the ones that aren't supposed to talk. I guess he's just for looks," Morris speculated. They turned around and watched the John Brown look-a-like amble down the street and go inside the fort.

As RVers, Morris and Edna never lingered too long in one particular place, always getting antsy to get going so they could see as much as possible. Today was no exception, and having felt they had exhausted the little that Harper's Ferry had to offer, climbed aboard and got on the road.

They were headed to Murfreesboro next, but they decided to take a little detour and drop in on some old friends they hadn't seen in many years. The friends were so surprised and excited, they begged the visitors to stay for a couple of days. Realizing that they needed to take a break from the road eventually, they decided to go ahead and do it now.

While they were there, the couple decided to drop their film they had used so far at a drug store. The following day they picked up their pictures so they could show their friends. The pictures from Antietam had come out especially well, as had the Gettysburg photos.

When they got to the Harper's Ferry photos, they weren't as pleased. The pictures of the fort had turned out just fine, but the pictures they really wanted to show their friends were the ones they had taken of the John Brown look-a-like. The pictures were there, but he wasn't in them.

Morris was ready to go give the drug store a piece of his mind, but Edna decided to check out the negatives. She flipped through until she got to the Harper's Ferry photos and then held the strips up one by one to the light. There was the fort, there they were, but no John Brown. They had snapped several pictures of him, yet he did not appear in any of the negatives or in the photos. Assuming it to be a camera glitch, they chalked those pictures off as a loss and moved on, never for a moment thinking it was odd that every other picture came out okay.

"I guess my eyes aren't what they used to be," Morris said, and left it at that.

The travelers finished their Civil War tour a few weeks later and returned home. They were glad to be home, but knew it was only a matter of time before they were up and on the road again.

They were right. They were invited to a wedding in West Virginia and having nothing better to do and a severe case of wanderlust, they packed up and hit the road.

It was a night wedding, and they had gotten such an early start, they decided to stop off and eat at the charming little restaurant they had found in Harper's Ferry. They exchanged pleasantries with some locals, explaining that this was not their first visit to Harper's Ferry.

"Last year we went on a whirlwind Civil War tour and this was our fourth stop," the woman explained.

"We especially loved the John Brown look-a-like. Too bad I screwed up the pictures that we took—we would have loved to compare the look-a-like with the genuine article," the old man said.

The man they were talking to looked at them strangely.

"What exactly was wrong with your pictures?" he asked suspiciously.

"Well the pictures are there, he's just not in it," Edna said. "Strange, isn't it?"

The man nodded absently and wished them a good day and safe travels. He considered telling them, but knew he would come off sounding silly if he actually tried to convince them of what he knew to be true. As a long-time resident of Harper's Ferry, he knew there was no John Brown look-a-like, and this was by no means the first time that a sighting had occurred. Old John Brown had vanished from many a tourist's photo-op.

"So old John Brown's at it again. Too bad," the man thought. So few people get a chance to see a ghost. These folks had a once-in-a-lifetime experience and didn't even know it.

As he walked toward his car, he glanced around, hoping to catch a glimpse of the old abolitionist, wandering the streets, reliving his stunning but brief brush with power. He didn't see him that day, but the man knew that he would come back. He always did.

The Singing Ghosts

The Singing Ghosts

You let me know if I can get you anything, ma'am," the landlord said. "Rent's due on the first and my door's always open to my tenants. Just let me know if you have any problems."

"Thank you very much. I'm sure I'll settle in here quite nicely," Ruth Wilson replied.

The landlord whistled as he walked away. He was really pleased with himself for finding such an ideal tenant. The old lady seemed sweet enough, and she was sure to be a quiet tenant that paid on time and didn't cause him too much trouble. In other words, she was a lot better than a lot of the drunks and ne'er-do-wells that he had had to contend with being a landlord in New Orleans.

Ruth looked around in her apartment. She liked it. Apparently it was built in the 1800s, but it had gone through some transformations since then. The old house used to be all one residence, and then it was occupied by Union troops when they controlled New Orleans. Later it became a factory, and now it was a boarding house. It had been remodeled nicely, with all the little details you expect from an older place, and was just enough space for her, living alone and all.

She put the kettle on her hot plate she had brought with her and settled by the window to sew. She was sewing a christening gown for her third grandchild. She should have been unpacking, but her old bones were already tired from relocating. The boxes could wait for her children or grandchildren to come help her.

She hummed to herself while she sewed and thought, "If these walls could talk..."

If those walls could have talked, they could have told her quite a story. She knew the Union army had occupied this house during the Civil War, but she did not know that it had a particularly strange history.

General Butler was in charge of the Union troops that occupied New Orleans. Looting is a problem in most wars, and this war was no exception. Trying to curtail the violence and infighting that looting can breed, he issued a strict mandate that any soldier caught looting would be shot. Apparently two soldiers either thought he was bluffing or thought they wouldn't get caught. Either way, they were caught red-handed looting an abandoned house in the French Quarter and were hauled off to the grand house, now Ruth's home, for their crime.

What those in power didn't know, however, was that these two were not actually Union soldiers—they were Confederate deserters in disguise. The two never really thought that the General would have two perfectly good "Union" soldiers shot. What a waste that would be! No, he was just trying to scare them a little.

They were in high spirits when they got to the temporary jail, so they bribed a guard to get them a bottle of liquor, which they consumed with a quickness. Soon they were laughing and carousing and caterwauling a popular Northern song called "John's Brown Body," hoping that the Yankee tune would ensure that their true identities would never be known.

They kept this behavior up around the clock, getting drunk and singing the same old song. Then they got the bad news. It seems that the anti-looting decree applied to all soldiers, Union or Confederate, and it had not been issued as a threat. Somehow they managed to find two pistols and on the night before they were to be tried, they shot each other in the chest.

Had Ruth known the macabre tale, she would have been nonplussed. She was a salty old lady who had seen too much of the world to be terrified by a silly old ghost story.

The kettle began to whistle, so Ruth heaved her old bones out of her rocking chair and made a cup of tea. She blew gently on the steaming cup of tea and gazed out the window at her new view. She had been born and raised in New Orleans and loved the city with all her heart. After her husband died she couldn't bear to stay in a house full of so many memories, so she cleaned out the house and moved to Constance Street.

As Ruth was admiring the view, she heard the sounds of rowdy singing on the floor above her. She grimaced when she heard it. The place was so nice, but what good was it if drunkards kept you up all night with their excessive noise. She waited to see if it would stop, and when it didn't, she took her broom and knocked the handle against the ceiling.

"That did the trick," she said happily, and returned to her tea. The sun was going down and the evening's first partygoers were filtering out of the woodwork. She took that as her cue to put herself to bed, turning off the lights and snuggling under the goose down comforter her grandmother had made for her.

About two o'clock in the morning, the old lady was awoken from her slumber by singing. "Oh no, they're at it again," she thought. They were even louder this time, singing in robust but slurring voices.

55

It sounded like the "Battle Hymn of the Republic." Of all the stupid songs to be singing at two in the morning, she thought.

The broom trick didn't work this time, so Ruth called her landlord. When she voiced her complaint, he mumbled knowingly, "Oh yeah, the singing," and then said something sleepily about taking care of it. She thought it was odd that he knew about this problem and failed to mention it to her. "Can't trust anybody these days," she thought to herself.

Whatever the landlord did apparently worked though, and she managed to get a good night's sleep after that.

Ruth awoke the next morning, yawned, stretched, and put the kettle on. While she waited for the water to heat she picked up the sewing she had left by her rocking chair. She carefully threaded the needle, noting that each time it got a little harder to do. She had slowly begun to stitch a hem when the singing started again.

This time it was really loud. She could hear the words and everything: "John Brown's body lies a-mouldering in the grave, John Brown's body lies a-mouldering in the grave, but his soul is marching on." She thought the melody was the "Battle Hymn of the Republic," but the words were very intelligible despite being slurred.

56

"Why don't you at least learn a new song," Ruth yelled in the direction of the singing, hammering her broom handle into the ceiling, to no avail. She made a call to the landlord, who was conveniently unavailable.

"I reckon I better get used to it," she said with a sigh, and reluctantly picked up her sewing, casting a disapproving and peevish glance toward the raucous singing every few minutes.

As quickly as it had started, the singing stopped.

"Well that's a relief," she thought to herself and took a few contented rocks in her chair. She wondered how long she would have to put up with all that racket. As it turned out she didn't have to wait much longer at all.

Ruth was rocking gently and stitching some lace onto the sleeve of the dress when she noticed the spot of blood on her hand. Ordinarily a careful seamstress, she was surprised. She didn't remember poking herself with the needle.

"Getting senile, are we old girl?" she thought to herself. She wiped off the spot of blood, grateful that it hadn't gotten on the beautiful fabric she was using to make the gown.

This time she felt it, a drip. Then another. She looked up and gasped in horror. Directly above her the ceiling was dripping fresh red blood, a small stain at first but quickly growing bigger. It looked like it was seeping through from the room above her. She jumped to her feet, dropping the tiny white dress into the puddle of blood that was beginning to form at her feet.

As quickly as she could, she was down the stairs and out the door, screaming all the way. She called her landlord and the police in hysterics from a pay phone. She waited for them outside the building but did not dare go back inside. They did a search of the place and came back out.

"I didn't see any blood," the landlord said with a condescending expression that implied she was just some crazy old coot. She didn't appreciate it. She may not have been a spring chicken, but she still had her wits about her.

"But what about the upstairs tenants? I know something horrible must have happened up there," Ruth said in frustration and disbelief.

"Look, lady. I'll level with you. Nobody's lived up there since the war, and by the war I mean the Civil War. Coupla soldiers shot themselves up there and since then people have seen and heard some pretty strange stuff. I didn't wanna scare you off, but that's the truth. Believe it or not."

Oh, she believed it alright. Somehow, she knew he was telling the truth. The singing, the blood, she knew it was not just her imagination.

"I'm breaking my lease and moving out. Charge me what you will. I'm not setting foot back inside that place. There is death living in that house," she said.

Ruth asked her children to move out her boxes because she refused to return to the room. Good thing she hadn't even had a chance to unpack.

Her children didn't believe her, of course. They expressed concern and urged her to have Alzheimer's tests done, convinced that she had dementia at the very least.

But then her son, leaving the apartment with the last load of his mother's things, happened to look up to the third floor from the sidewalk. He never told anyone, but through the window he saw two ragged men in Civil War uniforms, swaying clumsily and singing an unfamiliar tune.

The Haunted Honeymoon

The Haunted Honeymoon

Take your next left, and it should be right there on the right," Joe Sawyer, a young newlywed, said.

"Even if the hotel isn't there, we're getting out of this car. My legs are killing me," Anna, his bride, said, but she wasn't really complaining. She was still basking in the glow of her dream wedding. It had gone off without a hitch, and they had two full weeks of vacation to travel around.

They had thought about Jamaica, the Virgin Islands, Hawaii, all the typical honeymoon spots. Then they decided to keep it simple. They had never even seen all there was to see in their own country. Why not save a little money to use as a down payment on a house and just hit the road? Both of them were pretty low-maintenance, laid-back people, so the prospect sounded great to them.

They wanted to head west first, so they looked online and found a beautiful bed and breakfast in Vicksburg. They read up on the history of the war and decided the battlefield would be the first stop on their sight-seeing road trip.

Vicksburg had been a very important stronghold

for the south, especially due to its prime location on the Mississippi River. Capturing Vicksburg was of utmost importance to the Union agenda, so they really cut loose on the city. The people of Vicksburg had had a rough time as General Ulysses S. Grant's troops hammered them from the east and General William Tecumseh Sherman from the west. The city held out much longer than expected, however. Vicksburg was under siege for two months, receiving a constant bombardment of fire from the Union cannons and the gunboats on the river.

During this time the people of Vicksburg were completely cut off, some of them moving into caves for safety, some eating rats for lack of food, many of them dying of starvation and disease. By the time General Pemberton finally surrendered to the Union army on July 4, 1863, the city was completely devastated.

After reading all of that, the newlyweds were surprised that the bed-and-breakfast even survived the war. They were excited about staying in such a unique and storied place.

They both gasped when they pulled up in the circular drive. It was even more beautiful than the online photos led them to believe it was. The lawns were exquisitely manicured and the old-fashioned glass windows glittered in the late afternoon sun. The staff was attentive and informative, giving them a brief tour of the common areas before showing them to the honeymoon suite.

They followed their tour guide into a sitting room, and the groom noticed an amazing sight: a cannonball embedded in the parlor wall.

"Wow," Joe said, "it's amazing this place even made it through the war!"

"It's amazing that anything in Vicksburg made it. We assume that this place made it because it was eventually lucky enough to be used as a hospital for the Union army," the guide explained.

"Can't say I blame them for choosing this one," Anna said, admiring the gilded mirrors and tasteful décor.

"If anyone was brought here, the last things they cared about were aesthetics. They were probably worried about losing an arm or leg to the saw. Not to put a damper on your special day, and I'm sure you'll be quite comfortable here, but many wounded soldiers passed through the doors of this place."

"That just makes it all the more special," Joe beamed, putting his arm around his bride and kissing her on the cheek.

They were shown to their room and immediately fell in love with it. The suite was fantastic. "Wow, we really made a good choice on this place," Anna said to her husband after the porter had dropped off their bags and quietly shut the door. Every little detail was just so charming.

The wedding had been wonderful but exhausting, and after all that travel they were beat. They fell to sleep quite easily on the huge, fluffy down comforter that covered their tall, antique bed.

Joe was awakened in the middle of the night by heavy footsteps. Well, hotels are full of people, the good hotels anyway, so he wrote it off. He stepped into the little bathroom and had only been inside for a minute when he heard his wife crying. She was sobbing; what in the world could be the matter?

He finished his business as quickly as possible and stepped back into the bedroom. He was puzzled to see his wife sleeping soundly. He was confused; it really did sound like it was coming from right in the bedroom. He shook his head and crawled back into bed, falling back to sleep almost immediately.

A short time later Joe awoke again, this time from a rustling sound in the room. He rubbed his eyes with his knuckles and squinted to see where it was coming from. Near the foot of the bed a woman in a long black dress was folding sheets. He could barely make out her hair, pulled back in a low bun, and her facial expression, which looked pained and exhausted. As his eyes adjusted he could see dark circles beneath her eyes and her hollowed, sunken cheeks. What in the world was a maid doing in here at this hour?

Joe was just about to politely ask her to leave when he heard a cry of anguish. The woman in the black dress turned abruptly toward the sound of the scream, the bathroom, and immediately hurried there.

By this point, the young groom was getting a little creeped out. What kind of nuthouse was this hotel? He couldn't figure out why anyone would be in his bathroom, let alone why they might be screaming.

"That's it," he said putting on his bathrobe and angrily jumping out of bed. The shifting of the mattress woke his young bride, who watched him stalk into the bathroom.

"What's wrong, honey?" Anna asked him as he slowly walked back into the bedroom, "You look awful! Do you feel okay?"

Her husband said nothing, just furrowed his brow.

"Honey, what is it? Are you sick or something?"

"No, not sick," he said absently, "just had a weird dream, that's all. Sorry to wake you up." He sat on the edge of the bed but did not lie down.

"Are you coming back to bed?" the bride asked.

"Yeah, in just a minute. Good night," he said emptily.

"Good night," she murmured, already on her way back to sleep.

Joe didn't dare tell Anna what he had seen. First, the maid he had seen was not in the bathroom, even though he was almost positive he had seen her walk through the door. Second, he was sure he had a heard a scream come from the bathroom, but no screamer was to be found. Third, he could have sworn he saw blood on the floor. His eyes had adjusted enough to see it as he fumbled for the light switch, but when he turned on the light it was gone. He must have been sleepwalking—or that's what he was telling himself anyway.

Still, he was going to file a complaint about the maid coming in his room while they were asleep. He tried to go back to sleep but found himself growing more and more frightened, keeping one eye on the foot of the bed and the other on the bathroom door. He didn't sleep a wink.

The next morning Joe got up as soon as he heard signs of life outside of his room. He got dressed and stepped outside to talk to hotel management. He found a manager leaving the kitchen.

"I'm sorry, sir. We're still preparing breakfast but would you like a cup of coffee?"

"No thank you, I'm fine," he answered. "However, I

did want to ask somebody about a strange incident that occurred in our suite last night.

"Oh no! We pride ourselves on being a masterfully run establishment. I hope we can clear it up for you."

Joe told the management that a maid had been in his room last night folding linens. He knew she was just doing her job and didn't want her to get in trouble, he just thought management might want to know about the unorthodox behavior.

The woman looked at him strangely and said in a curt voice, "Sir, our maids go off duty at six o'clock every evening. There is simply no way there was a maid in your room. Perhaps you were dreaming?"

There is nothing more frustrating than not being believed, but he decided not to press the issue. He knew what he had seen. He had seen a ghost.

He returned to the room to wake up Anna so they could eat breakfast. The smell of the cooking bacon was delicious and he was anxious to eat, then to get back on the road.

When he got back to the room there was no need to wake up his new wife. She was sitting bolt upright in bed with her blankets pulled up to her chin. Her eyes were as big as saucers as she sat frozen with a fixed look at the bathroom door.

He knew what she was going to say before she said

it. The ghostly specter of the Civil War nursemaid had returned.

"Honey, oh my gosh," she said tentatively, "you probably won't believe me, but the strangest thing just happened…"

Old Green Eyes

Old Green Eyes

The bedraggled group of Confederates greeted each other, slapping backs and shaking hands. The small company of Southern soldiers was putting on its uniforms, milling about the campfire, and catching up on old times. The only things that seemed out of place were the long row of cars and trucks that had brought them to the battle.

These were Civil War re-enactors, not of the "hardcore" variety, but the type that borders on being known as "farbs." That's re-enactor slang for poseurs. These guys enjoyed getting together a few times a year, drinking beer, showing off pictures of their kids, and basically getting to play "war" on a grand scale. Think "Cowboys and Indians," only instead of a few kids in the backyard, it's hundreds of men on an actual battlefield.

This particular company had been meeting at Chickamauga Battlefield to re-enact the battle for years. In their regular lives these men were middle-aged, middle-class, regular guys. They just had a rather unique hobby on the weekends.

They knew the particulars of the battle like the

back of their hands. They knew that on September 19 and 20 of 1863, both sides fought for Chattanooga, an important railroad hub and a centrally important city to the Confederacy. It was a brutal and bloody battle, often resulting in hand-to-hand combat. The Rebels eventually won the battle after General James Longstreet led an offensive push through the Union line, after which they succeeded in basically routing the Union forces.

However, they certainly had their share of casualties. After the battle was over, 34,624 men had fallen. It was always amazing to the re-enactors that so many young men were killed in just two days. It was partly out of respect for all of that mortality that they returned to re-enact the battle each and every year.

The Confederate re-enactors loved Chickamauga especially, seeing as how they got to win every year. Yes, it was a lot more fun to be on the winning team.

To an outside spectator, it might seem odd to see a group of bearded men in soiled clothing and hobnail boots polishing Civil War muskets while they discussed the internet and commercial air travel, but most of the people who had shown up to see the re-enacted battle were Civil War buffs themselves who saw nothing out of the ordinary in the scene. Women

73

in field dresses and snoods strolled throughout the campsite while kids scampered about in mock conflict.

When the participants in this group learned that they would be members of Longstreet's brigade, they let forth a whoop of celebration. Not only did they get to be the winners today, they got to be some of the heroes that made it happen. The dramatic breach in Rosencrans' line was one of the most exciting events depicted in the battle.

The men mopped their brows with old-fashioned handkerchiefs and swilled beer from bottles. It was a scorcher of a day, and while their wool uniforms might be well-ventilated, but they were still blazingly hot. They had done all the catching up they wanted to do and were ready for "battle." They were ready to get the show on the road.

Eventually, the ragtag group of Confederates was herded into place for the battle to begin. They heard the action getting started over by Jay's Mill, the site where the actual fighting had begun.

Soon the men were into the action and found themselves, as always, getting really into it with Rebel Yells, cries of pain, and anguish at the sight of a fallen comrade. It was all in good fun, but it was powerful to the men as well. They knew that only blanks were being shot, their fallen friends were just taking a breather, and they would all ride home in their air-conditioned cars at the end of the day. However, their imaginations were powerful enough that participating in the re-enactment truly helped them understand at least how the battle would have looked to a soldier, if not how it felt.

The time came for the great climax, and the remaining men made ready for their fierce assault. They could all see the pre-arranged chink in the Union line's armor, and, screaming bloody murder, they hurtled across the field to attack.

As they engaged the Union soldiers they recognized re-enactment regulars with whom they'd done battle before. Ordinarily they would have exchanged pleasantries, but now was not the time. They fired blanks at each other, some falling to their deaths, some battling on valiantly.

Soon the routing of Rosencrans's army was complete. At this point in the battle General George Thomas took command of the Union troops who remained. The re-enactors watched as he formed his line on Snodgrass Hill. Although he definitely had an upper hand being on top of a hill, he led his meager troops with great valor and tenacity. Due to his ability to maintain control of the hill despite the constant onslaught of Rebel fire, he earned the nickname "the Rock of Chickamauga."

The re-enactors were part of this onslaught, and they participated with great relish. They charged toward the hill with their muskets ready. The first wave of "bullets" dropped some of the men to their knees. One re-enactor caught an especially accurate fall in his periphery; he reminded himself to congratulate his comrade on his technique as soon as they returned to camp.

Eventually most of their group had fallen, as pre-arranged around the campfire. One soldier, however, veered off from the rest of the group and into the woods near Snodgrass Hill. He wasn't a deserter—it was Charles Morgan, and he just very urgently needed to go to the bathroom. All of the beer he had drunk before the battle caught up with him during Longstreet's charge, and this was his first opportunity to slip off and take care of it. As he leaned against a tree he closed his eyes and listened to the sharp cracking of the musket blanks, the trumpets blaring and the drums banging, the yells of triumph and pain, and smiled to himself. He hadn't had this much fun since the last re-enactment.

Behind him, all of a sudden, Charles heard the crunch of leaves underfoot. Expecting a Yankee "sniper," he pulled out his bayonet, turned around quickly and said playfully, "Hold it right there, Billy Yank!"

His dramatic monologue was cut short, however. He was frozen solid as he gazed upon the source of sound. It was lucky for him he had just relieved himself or he might have done it right there.

About ten yards away, though backlit by the sun, there stood a huge, hulking figure. Charles could see that the creature was covered in coarse, wiry hair from head to toe. Charles was frozen, hypnotized by the eyes that gazed upon him. The eyes were blazingly green, glowing sinister and fiery as if they were lit from within. The creature held him with his gaze for some time; the re-enactor couldn't have said how long. It felt like an eternity. The sounds of the re-enactment faded into the distance; all he could hear was the sound of his own heart beating.

Charles raised a shaking hand in tentative greeting. The hulking behemoth slowly turned his back to the man and lumbered off slowly into the woods. It wasn't until the monster was out of sight that he realized he was trembling. He took a deep breath and hurried on wobbly legs out of the woods and back into the fray.

By the time the battle had ended, everyone in his company was back at the campfire relating their favorite parts of the battle. They were all laughing and talking at once, poking fun at one another's performances and admiring others. Charles straggled in, his face devoid of expression. His buddy clapped him on the back and said, "What's the matter, Johnny Reb? You look like you seen a ghost."

"I didn't see a ghost," Charles said quietly, "I saw Old Green Eyes, I swear to God. I saw him."

His company all groaned collectively. The legend of Old Green Eyes went all the way back to the actual battle. Supposedly soldiers on Snodgrass Hill had seen him creeping around in the trees on two legs, covered in hair, with glowing green eyes. In other words, the legend looked exactly like what the re-enactor had seen. Then the company all laughed at what they assumed to be a prank, waiting for their fellow soldier to crack a smile. He never did.

"I don't care if you believe me; I know what I saw," Charles said quietly and a little defensively.

"Oh come on, buddy," one of them tried to say, "you know re-enactors are prone to tell some tall tales and that's fine. That's part of what makes it fun. But Old Green Eyes? Come on."

Charles told everyone to just forget he ever said anything. He collected his things, changed into street clothes, said goodbye, and drove away. As he pulled out of the battlefield, he couldn't get the image of the monstrosity he had seen out of his head. He closed his eyes briefly and shook his head quickly, turned the stereo up full blast, and tried to forget what he knew he had seen.

His fellow Confederates reunited once again around a campfire at Chickamauga the following year, but Charles was not among the graybacks who re-enacted the battle that day. He never forgot his strange encounter with Old Green Eyes; thus, he never returned to Chickamauga again as long as he lived.

Spook Hill

Spook Hill

The tired couple literally fell into their small rental car. Although both of them were in pretty good shape, the Maryland portion of the Appalachian Trail had really taken the wind out of their sails.

They sat for a moment without moving, heads against headrests, eyes closed. Then they slowly turned their heads toward each other, opened their eyes, and exchanged a small smile. The look in their eyes said it, "I'm tired, I'm hungry, but I'm happy."

"We did it," the young woman, Jane, said quietly.

"Yeah," Russell, her husband, said contentedly. Neither was feeling particularly eloquent at the moment, but those few words said all they wanted to say.

They had just recently gotten into hiking, so they still didn't have the endurance to take on the entire trail—far from it, in fact. They had lugged their packs through most of a portion of the Maryland section of the Trail, which was only a small and relatively easy part of the daunting Appalachian Trail, but they were beginners who were pleased with this little victory. First a bit of Maryland, then all of it, then on down into West Virginia. Who knew, maybe one day they would start in Maine and go the whole nine yards, which was really more like 2,000 miles.

"So how about the whole thing? Think we'll be ready next year?" Jane asked her husband.

Russell chuckled and replied, "Maybe in our next life. Ready to head out?" Their packs stowed safely in the rear portion of their car, they pulled their tired legs into the car, buckled up, and headed out.

The country here in the hills of Maryland was beautiful, so the couple decided to take a few more days to see some of it by car, giving their legs a much deserved rest.

What these ambitious hiking upstarts didn't know was that they had been hiking and driving on and around the ridge of South Mountain. The beautiful foliage and breathtaking views were a visual feast for the nature buffs, but history enthusiasts had an interest in the area that was quite different.

A Civil War battle occurred at South Mountain, a battle that immediately preceded Antietam. That was probably why the young couple had no idea that they were even on or around a historic site; Antietam, located in Sharpsburg, Maryland, overshadowed this smaller battle, although it was strategically important and the death toll significant.

Robert E. Lee, the legendary Confederate general, had decided to go on the offensive and invade the North. The battle started on September 14, although it would be more accurate to say "battles." They were fighting over three different mountain gaps: Crampton's Gap, Fox's Gap, and Turner's Gap. As a result, both armies were somewhat scattered and confused. Lee eventually retreated, and a few days later came Antietam.

This Maryland battle may be overshadowed by the larger, later battle of Antietam, but legends still survive.

One of these legends is that in order to gain the upper hand, the Confederates had decided to move their cannons to the top of a hill, separating them from the Yankees. They would do so quietly and in cover of night, and when morning came, the Confederates could slaughter the surprised and unprepared Union soldiers. They pushed and pulled the heavy armaments up the grade, trying to do so as quickly and quietly as possible. Little did they know, the jig was up.

Union scouts had seen what the Rebels were up to. The Yanks quickly but quietly made their way to the top of the hill, leaving heavy and cumbersome equipment behind. When they crested the hill, they beat the Rebels at their own game by firing on them. The Rebels were just as they had hoped the Yankees

84

would be: surprised and unprepared. They were picked off like fish in a barrel and suffered many losses that night.

The young couple knew none of this however, and as they drove along the mountain road they were astounded by the incredible beauty of the Appalachians. They were glad they had decided to rough it a little on their anniversary instead of just lying around on a beach somewhere. They had never been to this part of the country before, and now that they were here, they realized they didn't know what they were missing.

After driving for some time, they checked the map and figured that they were approaching a town called Burkittsville. As they passed the sign that read, "Welcome to the historic village of Burkittsville, 1825," Jane thought it looked familiar.

"Say, isn't this where that Blair Witch documentary or movie or whatever took place? I could have sworn it was Burkittsville. I think it was the same sign," she said interestedly.

"Hmm. Good thing we already stopped for gas," Russell said with a wink.

"I think we should stop for the night," Jane suggested. "It's not like we're gonna find anything else interesting way out here in the middle of nowhere."

"Alright, Burkittsville, it is. Only don't wake me up when you get all freaked out," Russell said teasingly.

They pulled into the sleepy little town and slowly cruised down the street. They didn't really see much in the way of lodging, but a local suggested they try Franklin. There were all kinds of affordable hotels over in Franklin. He also suggested they check out the Gathland State Park while they were so close, a park which was situated in Crampton's Gap.

They thanked the man and rolled up the window.

"Wanna check it out?" Russell asked his wife.

"I'm pretty tired, but we might as well. Either way I'm gonna sleep like a log tonight," Jane replied with a yawn.

Following the local's directions, they drove out of town on Gapland Road. They admired the pastoral vistas in the late afternoon sun.

They passed a barn and began to crest a hill. Admiring the view from the top, Jane asked, "What was the name of this road again?"

"I was just wondering the same thing myself. Gapland Road or something. Come to think of it, I'm not sure if this is exactly the way that guy told us to go."

"Oh, ha ha ha," Jane said sarcastically with a wry smile, "you're such a liar. You think I'm gonna get all

86

freaked out because we're lost near the woods and the Blair Witch is gonna get me and leave weird stuff outside your tent and blah, blah, blah. C'mon, hon, you can do better than that, can't you?" she asked with a smirk.

"No, really," Russell said as they coasted over the hill. "I really think we're going the wrong way."

Jane just sighed and shook her head bemusedly as she realized that they were coasting to a stop at the bottom of the hill.

Russell shifted the car into neutral and pulled the map out from the glove compartment. He furrowed his brow and began to look for the name of the road they were on. It was always so hard to find these little country roads, not to mention the fact that he was lousy with a map.

"Exactly how long do you plan to keep this little charade up?" Jane asked, a little annoyed this time. "Honey, I'm tired and hungry and more than a little bit…why are you driving backwards?"

"What are you talking about?" Russell mumbled, still studying the map in his lap.

"You obviously have your foot on the gas and the car in reverse or something," Jane said quickly, looking over her shoulder and up the hill to make sure no other cars were coming.

Russell glanced up quickly, looked back at his map, and then looked up again. He cocked his head with a look of bewilderment as a speed limit sign passed behind his wife's head.

He looked quickly at his feet, which rested flat on the floor nowhere near the gas or brake. With his right hand he jiggled the gear shift, which swung idly back and forth in neutral.

All the while they moved not only backward, but uphill.

"Stop it, Russell," Jane said in a panicked voice. "Someone's gonna come flying over that hill and nail us!"

"I'm not doing it! I swear! Look," he said, and jammed his foot onto the brake pedal. The movement slowed slightly, but slowly continued its gravity-defying movement in reverse.

"What is going on?" he said in frustration and a little bit of panic.

"Here, I'll get in the driver's seat, you push the car down," Jane tried to say calmly, though she realized how crazy it sounded.

"Good idea," Russell said, and jumped out of the car. It wasn't moving terribly fast, but this defied all logic. As he trotted around to the rear of the car he shook his head and thought about how strange it was to be pushing a car down a hill instead of up.

"Hit the gas! I'm gonna push," Russell called, trying to disguise the bewilderment and growing panic in his voice.

Jane did just that, and he hefted all of his body weight against the bumper. He felt the car move slightly downhill, but as soon as he stopped pushing, it began creeping up again.

"Oh, come on," he said and slammed his body into the rental car. He gritted his teeth and strained, letting forth the pained sound of a man exerting all of his physical strength. Jane gunned the engine, and looked into the rearview mirror in a growing panic, praying she didn't see an eighteen-wheeler barreling over the hill and straight into the rear of their oncoming car.

Finally, as if exhausted from resisting, the car started to slowly accelerate downhill. It picked up speed not from restored gravity alone, but Jane's defiantly heavy foot on the gas as well.

"Thank God," Russell thought as he trotted down the hill alongside the road.

"I kept it in first and put on the emergency brake," Jane said when her husband returned to the car, shaky and out-of-breath from running on tired legs and pushing a stubborn car. "I say we go straight to a hotel."

"Fine by me," the winded young husband said as he flopped into the passenger seat, "you're driving."

They rode in silence for a few minutes, neither wanting to be the first to broach the subject of the strange phenomena they had just experienced. Russell turned up the radio which had been playing softly since they left the hike.

"So, um, that was pretty weird," he said finally.

"Yeah," Jane said quickly, as if she had been waiting for him to say something, anything. Neither really knew what to say, but those few words seemed to be enough.

They didn't bother to stop and relate what had happened to any local residents for fear of not being believed. Maybe they were just loopy from the hike, they thought.

Had they stopped and told their story, however, the young couple might have felt a little better. Well, at least they would have known they weren't both simultaneously going crazy or gravity didn't momentarily stop working. For what they didn't know was that that hill, known to some as "Spook Hill," was the very one over which the Confederate soldiers had attempted to muscle their cannons in silence, only to be swiftly cut down by the Union soldiers who had crept up the other side.

What local residents believed was that each and every day, if you paused at the bottom long enough to let the Rebel soldiers get a good hold on your car, they'd push that piece of equipment right up that hill, struggling valiantly against the gravity that wished to push it down. About halfway up the hill, however, about where they were when the Union troops had opened fire, they would release their burden and let it fall, just as they had released their souls and let them fly. On they pushed, day in, day out, just like Sisyphus. Maybe one of these days they'll finally make it to the top. Would you like to help them try?

Lost Souls of Pea Patch Island

Lost Souls of Pea Patch Island

I f you kids would just sit still for one second, we'll get this over with," the mother said, adjusting the focus and squinting through the view finder. "I know y'all hate having your picture taken, but one day you'll thank me."

"Yeah, right," said Steve. He was at that self-conscious age during which the last thing on earth you want is to pose in front of historical landmarks like an idiot with your kid brother. The only thing he would have wanted to do less was take this stupid trip in the first place.

"C'mon, Steve. Eight days of being stuck with your family down, two to go. You can make it," his dad said, a hint of exasperation in his voice. He had hoped that taking a family road trip might bring them all a little closer together. The past few years they had been at odds with Steve more and more, who only grew more and more distant. Chalking it up to adolescence was about all they had to cling to.

Having been to Boston and Philadelphia to see all the sights, the Bradleys decided to make a trip to Pea Patch Island, a small island in the Delaware River near the entrance to Delaware Bay. They made the short ferry trip out to the island and took a tour. They were currently having their pictures begrudgingly taken in front of Fort Delaware, which the tour guide explained was built in 1814 in order to protect Philadelphia and surrounding areas.

The tour guide had also explained that during the Civil War, Pea Patch Island had been used as a camp for Confederate prisoners. Wooden barracks had been hastily constructed to accommodate the prisoners, but they did little to protect them from the elements, particularly the cold. The climate of the island was a bit marshy as well, leading to chronically damp conditions and the health problems they breed. Crowding became a problem after Gettysburg, when the prison population swelled to nearly seventeen thousand. In other words, no matter how miserable Steve may have been on Pea Patch Island with his family, there were others who had been there before him who had had it much, much worse.

"Okay, you two are free from pictures for the time being. Your mother and I are gonna walk around for a little bit," his father, Eric, said. "Steve, keep an eye on your little brother, okay?"

"Why don't you keep an eye on him?" Steve grumbled under his breath.

"What's that, son?" his mother asked, raising one eyebrow. That was her "thin ice" expression.

"Nothing," Steve mumbled. He grabbed his brother by the hand and jerked him along behind him.

Steve wasn't sure why he was being so cranky. He actually kind of liked history—as much as he liked anything these days anyway. For now, though, the only thing he wanted was to sit by the water and be left alone.

They walked in the grass by the water's edge. Maybe after they did a lap, his parents would be ready to go. The island was only about a mile long, after all.

He found a somewhat isolated spot and plopped down in the grass. His brother plopped down beside him.

"Wanna play a game?" his little brother, Timothy, asked hesitantly. His big brother hadn't been very nice to him lately, and he certainly was never in the mood to play games anymore.

This time was no exception. Without a word, Steve pulled his iPod out of his pocket, jammed the ear buds in his ears, lay back on the grass, and closed his eyes.

Timothy sighed and looked out at the water. That got boring really quickly. He pulled a blade of grass out of the ground and wound it around his finger until it turned purple. He gently pulled up little clumps of grass and sprinkled them over his prostrate brother, who would immediately brush it off in a huff and tell him to "Knock it off."

Drawing his knees up underneath his little chin, he sighed and looked out at the water again. The sun glittered off the rippling river water and sparkled so much he had to squint his eyes to look at it.

Timothy assumed his parents would be along to get them soon. What he didn't know was that his parents were a bit relieved to have some time alone away from the kids, especially the brooding teenager. They had a ways to go yet before they could get some pizza and drive back to the hotel.

The longer they sat side by side on the riverbank, the more the wind picked up. Timothy squinted up at the sky and noticed some clouds forming. Yes, he noticed, the wind had really picked up. The clouds hung heavy and dark and ominous over the horizon.

"Surely they'll have to come get us now," he thought. He watched as the ripples were slowly becoming tiny waves. The tourists on the island were heading en masse back towards the ferry landing, and he was ready to be among them.

"Steve, Steve," the little boy said swatting him with the back of his hand.

"Knock it off, you little pest," Steve snarled. "Can't

you see I'm busy? Mom and Dad will take their sweet time and then come get us whenever they're ready. There's no point running around and looking for them now. Chill out, will ya?"

Heaving another sigh, Timothy turned back toward the water and observed the impending storm's effect on the water.

Suddenly, he thought he saw something in the swirling water. A turtle or something, maybe?

The steadily choppier water dipped slightly and the little boy saw it again. This time he gasped.

"Steve! Steve! Get up, Steve! There's someone in the water," the little boy cried, tugging frantically on his big brother's shirt.

"Shut up, you little brat. I told you to leave me alone until time to go back to the hotel."

"No really, Steve! There's somebody in the water! I think that he's drowning," the little boy said, feeling tears of panic welling up into his eyes. You're a big boy now, he told himself. Cut out all this crying business and do something.

With that bit of self-inspiration, he yanked Steve's ear phones out of his ears, grabbed the iPod, and held it out of his brother's reach. That got his attention for sure.

As Steve sat up in furious indignation, he saw

98

something funny out of the corner of his eye. The little brat was right—that did look like somebody might be drowning.

"Oh my gosh," Steve said, "you're right! We gotta do something. You stay here and try as hard as you can not to lose sight of them in the water. I'll be back!"

With that Steve dove in the water and began paddling over to the drowning person. His brother's lip quivered as he crouched by the water and watched a pair of pale hands flailing, reaching out to grab onto something, only there was nothing to grab onto.

Timothy rocked back and forth on his haunches and emitted a little whine of panic. He wished he had taken swimming lessons like his mom had wanted him to. What would he do if Steve wound up needing help too?

He watched as Steve drew up close to the flailing hands, hands whose fingers were gnarling and twisting in panic. Steve finally reached the person and reached out to grab the hand. Just as he was about to grab it, it seemed to disappear. He dove underwater and groped around blindly for the hand. It seemed strange that he couldn't feel anything, not a hand, arm, head, nothing. It was as if nothing was there.

All of a sudden Timothy shot up to his feet. He saw another set of bubbles appear beside the other drowning person. He was relieved when Steve resurfaced a moment later, gasping for breath, looking around him frantically for the drowning person.

Then, the little boy saw another set of pale hands pop up behind his brother, groping desperately for something stationary. All the while the impending storm rendered the water more and more hostile.

"They're not going to make it," the little boy thought. This grown-up thought shocked him a little bit as the mighty current churned around the upstretched hands, begging for help. Every time Steve lunged for the hands, they seemed to vanish.

Steve disappeared under water a few times more and then, exhausted, began his trip back to the shore. As he pulled himself up onto the bank with the help of his sobbing little brother, he panted, "I kept grabbing for them, but I couldn't get a hold. C'mon, let's go for help."

The pair of brothers ran as fast as they could back toward the ferry landing.

"Oh my gosh, Steve, are you okay?" his mother asked frantically, taking him into her arms. Steve nodded an exhausted "yes" and turned to a curious staff member. He breathlessly related to a staff member what had happened, explaining that every time he had tried to grab the panicked hands, they disappeared.

"We'll take care of it son, don't you worry," the staff member said soothingly. He sent another staff member off to tend to the emergency.

"But, but…," the little boy stopped short. He looked off into the distance but the hands were out of sight now.

"We want to thank you for being so observant and getting help right away. And you, young man," he said looking at Steve, "did a very brave thing." At this Steve blushed and nodded, the water dripping off of his soaked head.

"However, at this point we're going to have to ask you to clear the coastline and board the ferry. We need to give the rescue staff room to do what they need to do. Thank you again for everything, boys," the staff member said.

Lest their little boy be exposed to human mortality a little earlier than they had hoped, the parents put their arms around Timothy's shoulders and turned him gently toward the direction of the ferry. As they led him away, he kept turning and looking back.

Steve brooded silently, which was not out of the ordinary, but he, too, was affected by the hands he had seen floundering in the river. He couldn't help but think he failed. He had an odd feeling about all of this. He turned and glanced over his shoulder and saw the staff member staring out into the choppy water with his hands on his hips. When Steve had told him about seeing someone drowning in the bay, the man had reacted so calmly and without a trace of surprise.

There was a good reason for that.

"You boys will never learn," the man said quietly to the stormy river water.

Two Confederate prisoners of war had somehow escaped from their barracks and jumped, unnoticed into the choppy waters of the river one stormy day. Weakened by captivity and meager nutrition, they were no match for the Delaware that day. It wasn't until they were floundering and drowning in the powerful current that the Union guards even knew they were gone. They watched stonily from the riverbank until first one pair of hands, then another, then the last ones disappeared beneath the surface of the river. No sense risking their necks for some no-account, secessionist traitors anyway, they thought. After all signs of life had been covered by the waves of the river, they turned silently toward the fort and returned to their stations. This was a sad war, for comrade and enemy alike, they thought.

The attendant scanned the water for the Rebel soldiers, the would-be escapees, and saw nothing. What sad spirits they must be, he thought. Grasping and clutching for life-giving air and never getting it. Drowning for all eternity. The man shivered at this thought. Although he was a Union sympathizer whose ancestors fought for the North, he couldn't help thinking that he hoped that one day, those poor Rebel boys reached the other side.

The Trapped Ghost of Hopewell

The Trapped Ghost of Hopewell

Great, another old house," Rob thought to himself dully as he climbed the steps of the old antebellum home. For the life of him he couldn't figure out why his girlfriend was so into all this old stuff.

"Wow. What a cool place! I wonder how many people have walked up and down these stairs since it was built," Lydia thought to herself excitedly, a typical thought for her and exactly why she was so into all this old stuff.

She liked antique homes, antique stores, antique just-about-anything. She was a dreamy and imaginative girl who always believed she had been born in the wrong century. Something about the past had always intrigued her, and her imagination allowed her to enjoy everything it had to offer in the way of tours, classes, artifacts, graveyards, or just about any other relic you could think of.

Her boyfriend did not share this obsession with history. While she preferred the old gabled antiquity of an antebellum home, he preferred new, shiny, modern things, technology, the present, the future. It seemed that no matter where they went on a trip or off the beaten path, there was some old house or historic site that Lydia just had to see.

Sure enough, this road trip proved to be no different. At Lydia's insistence and persuasion, they had already had to pull off on the side of the road for every historical marker they passed. They stopped for lunch at a diner in Virginia, and lo-and-behold, there was a travel brochure for local historical attractions. Rob groaned inwardly, but he was not really surprised—even he knew that Virginia was chock full of history, particularly Civil War history, due to the state's proximity to enemy Union territory.

Lydia found a blurb about an antebellum house in nearby Hopewell and didn't have to try too hard to convince Rob to make the short trip. He made a half-hearted protest, but it was more teasing than serious. He decided to try to be a good sport about it as he drove toward the house, using a crude map scribbled on a diner napkin.

They found the house easily enough, parked, and walked up the stairs. A tour was beginning momentarily, and Lydia's eyes shone too excitedly for her boyfriend to refuse her.

"These tours are all alike," he sighed to himself as he leaned against the railing of the sprawling front porch. This was exactly the kind of thing Lydia liked about these old houses—sprawling front porches littered with rocking chairs, porch swings, and any other surface one could sit on and escape the sweltering summer heat.

At last the tour began and they filed into the old home. Their noses were immediately greeted by a smell that Lydia loved and Rob hated—the unmistakable smell of old stuff. Lydia hung on every word, but Rob lagged at the back, his hands in his pockets, his mind wandering. While Lydia oohed and ahhed at the antique furniture and décor, the warped floor boards and the faded fabrics, wishing that she could live in just such a house, Rob checked his watch, wishing that this tour would wrap up soon so they could get back in the road. He wanted to make it to Philadelphia in time to crash with some of his friends.

As the tour group turned down a hallway, Rob broke away from the group. Lydia gave him a puzzled look, and he mouthed the word "bathroom." She nodded and he drifted away from the crowd of eager history buffs.

In reality he wasn't looking for a bathroom. From his experiences of being dragged along on these little historical jaunts, the best way for him to deal with it was to break away from the group and give himself a tour, stopping only when he saw something that interested him in particular.

He soon found himself descending some low, narrow steps into what he guessed to be the basement. Maybe I'll find something creepy or interesting down there, he thought.

The air was stale and close and the basement dimly lit, so dimly lit in fact that the corners were pitch black. He gave the room a sweeping look, trying to see if there was anything worth noticing.

He was just about to give up when, all of a sudden, he heard a noise behind his back, causing him to jump. He was alone in the basement and the sounds of the tour above him had grown faint and distant, rendering the sound behind him all the more startling.

He looked quizzically at the wall behind him. Scratch, scratch, scratch, he heard coming from behind the wall. Is it a rat, he wondered, leaning a little closer. Yes, it was definitely a clawing sound coming from behind the wall. As quickly as it had started, it stopped.

Having decided that the scratching was being done by a rat or a squirrel or some other vermin, Rob began to turn to head back up the stairs. Then, again: scratch, scratch, scratch, louder this time. He turned back toward the noisy wall. He leaned in closer to it, examining it closely, running his fingers along the boards to see if he could find some sort of opening. That must be some rat, he thought to himself, as the scratching became more loud and frantic.

His gaze followed the sound of the scratching as it slid down to the wall and became silent. He tentatively put an ear to the wall near the baseboard, when all of a sudden, something began to thump slowly behind the wall, causing him to bolt upright. The thumping was weak, and was then accompanied by a sort of high-pitched whine.

"These old places must have all kinds of pest problems," he said to himself bravely, comfortingly. "That's why I prefer the modern stuff. Yes sirree, clean and efficient, that's the way I like it," he thought. Although the sound coming from behind the wall seemed much too loud and strong for a rat, it was the only logical explanation.

Then, as the thumping slowly turned back into the scratching, this time more halfhearted, his "logical explanation" flew out the window as he heard a low voice moaning behind the wall.

With that he turned and hurried up the stairs. As he ascended the stairs, he tried to tell himself that his quickened pace had nothing to do with whatever was clawing behind the wall.

He mounted the stairs and gave a quick, cursory look around. When he didn't see the tour group, he decided, somewhat relieved, to wait for Lydia on the porch. His run in with the giant mutant rat or whatever it was had caused his breath to become shallow, and besides, he needed some fresh air after the heavy, stale air of the basement.

Finally, Lydia drifted out of the front door with the other tourists. Rob smiled a little despite himself; he knew that enraptured look on her face. It would be hours before she snapped out of the romantic reverie.

"Oh, there you are. I guess we lost you," she said, "Did you find the bathroom?"

"What? Oh, yeah, the bathroom," he stammered, "I found it." Then he said in a tone that was more a statement than a question, "Ready to go?"

They strolled hand in hand toward the car.

"So what was your favorite part?" he prompted, knowing that such a response could easily kill thirty minutes of boredom on the road.

"Oh, I loved it all—surprise, surprise," she said, giving him a sidelong smile. "But I especially liked the basement."

"Wow, how cool, the basement," he said in a mildly sarcastic way, playing his assigned part in one of the comfortable routines of their relationship; but, he noticed that his hands tensed up a little on the steering wheel when she mentioned the basement.

She smacked him lightly on the arm. "No really, it was neat. I guess you missed that part of the tour."

"Well," she continued, "as you heard in the tour, the house has had its share of visitors over the years, especially because of the Civil War."

He nodded, blushing a little as he realized that he hadn't been paying attention to anything the tour guide had said.

"Well, there was this nurse who worked in the house who was a Union sympathizer, but of course she didn't tell anybody that. She heard the news that some Confederates were coming to the house to inspect it, so she hid this Union soldier behind a secret wall in the basement."

He felt the blood slowly drain from his face and the hairs on his arms began to rise.

"The Confederates showed up and found all kinds of Yankee paraphernalia in her storage space, so they accused her of being a traitor and hauled her off to prison somewhere."

He could already see where this was going.

"Well, nobody but the nurse knew about the Union soldier hidden behind the wall. He clawed and pulled at the wall, but to no avail. You could only open the wall up from the outside. So he died of dehydration, or malnourishment, or whatever it is you die of when you're stuck in a closed space. Can you imagine how awful that would be? It kinda reminds me of that Edgar Allen Poe short story."

He could hear the blood rushing in his ears as his girlfriend chattered on about the Union soldier trapped behind the wall.

"Then," she said in a way where he could tell she was about to get to the juicy part, the finale, "they were remodeling the basement in the fifties and they found his bones rotting away behind the walls. Isn't that wild? See, isn't history fascinating?" she asked rhetorically, contentedly.

He cleared his throat and tried to ask casually, "So, um, did you hear anything weird in the basement?"

"Weird? No," she said, "although the tour guide said something about how sometimes they supposedly hear the ghost of the Union soldier trying to claw his way out," she said theatrically, waving her hands in Rob's face.

"Oooh! How terrifying," he said in a silly way, trying to be playful. She didn't notice how forced it sounded.

I'm a reasonable guy, he thought to himself. What I heard in that basement was clearly just some kind of animal. Maybe, um, the house settling. Sure, that must have been it.

Rob tried to shake the maddening sensation of knowing he had experienced something but not wanting to admit it to himself. He relaxed his grip on the steering wheel as he saw that his knuckles were turning white and tried to think calmly.

He couldn't. His gut instinct had been right all along. That was no rat; he now knew it for sure. He also knew for sure, as he steered the car northward, that the next time Lydia wanted to go on one of her little historical trips, she could definitely count him out.

The Ghost of the Boy Hero

The Ghost of the Boy Hero

Shhh! We're gonna get caught," John whispered to his buddies, trying to suppress an excited giggle. They weren't exactly breaking the law, for Mount Holly Cemetery was open to the public until dusk, but preteens hanging around anywhere after dark were generally considered suspicious and frowned upon. Sooner or later a police officer would probably show up to ruin their fun.

The boys weren't even sure what they were hoping to find that night in the cemetery. Like all the kids in Little Rock, they had heard the urban legends and ghost lore surrounding the cemetery, of which there was plenty. A lot of Confederate soldiers and officers were buried there because after Vicksburg had fallen to the Union forces, Little Rock was not far behind.

"I heard you can see the ghosts of dead people floating around the graveyard," one of the boys whispered to his friends.

"Oh yeah, right," his friend said sarcastically. "Don't tell me you believe all that stuff about ghouls and ghosts. That's kid's stuff."

For all the detractor's bravado, however, he had to admit guiltily to himself that he did feel a twinge of nervousness. He also tried to forget that they weren't that much older than kids. They couldn't even drive yet; they had dropped their bikes at the rear of the cemetery and crept in on foot.

As they knelt behind an obelisk, they sent Matt, the bravest (or maybe the dumbest) of the bunch, on a scouting mission. He crouched over and scuttled from tombstone to tombstone, peeking out from around the stones that glowed in the moonlight. He thought maybe they were being a little overly precautious, but being sent on a mission lent an air of danger to their outing that he liked.

Deciding he would mess with his friends a little, he ducked behind a mausoleum and waited. When he didn't come back immediately, he knew they would come looking for him.

Sure enough, after some minutes had passed (it seemed like an eternity to both Matt and his increasingly anxious friends), the group decided that they should go and have a look.

They set out as a pack, not wanting to admit to each other that they wanted to stick as close together as possible.

"Matt?" they called out questioningly, raising their

voices just enough to carry but not so much as to arouse suspicion.

Matt didn't answer, biting his lip to hold back the laughter.

"Matt!" they called out a little louder this time, startling themselves with the volume of their voices in the deathly quiet graveyard.

Still Matt waited, covering his mouth with his hand as he heard their footsteps move closer, rustling the grass beneath their sneakers.

Just as they began to draw up beside the prankster's hiding place, Matt leapt out from behind the tombstone and screamed bloody murder.

A collective yelp escaped from all of the boys who instinctively jumped closer together. They stood wide eyed and shaking, gasping for breath. Matt collapsed on the ground in peals of laughter, holding his stomach and kicking his legs.

"You should have seen the looks on your faces," he gasped between fits of laughter.

The boys were glad that the furious red flushing their cheeks was not visible in the light of the moon. Their hearts pounded so loudly they were sure each one could hear the other.

"Shhhh," T.J. hissed angrily, "we'll get caught for sure with you making all that racket."

"Oh, don't be mad just because I got you," Matt said, his laughter subsiding to sporadic chuckles. "I was just having a little fun."

"You didn't scare me," Adam sniffed, trying to regain some of his wounded and still shaky pride.

"Oh, come off it," Matt replied. "You screamed like a little girl." With that he did an imitation of Adam's shrill shriek that sent him back onto the ground in a fit of giggles and his friends into a fit of shushing.

After Matt's laughter faded and his friends' composure was regained, they decided to play hide-and-go-seek. What better way to reassert their manhood than splitting up in a graveyard at night. One of them suggested playing in teams, a suggestion so transparently cowardly he regretted having said it the minute it crossed his lips. After another delay-of-game for the taunting the suggestion elicited, they finally got the game underway.

It was decided that a round of Rock-Paper-Scissors would be the most judicious way to determine who was "it," and in the end, Adam's rock beat T.J.'s scissors, leaving him to be the seeker.

"Ready, set, go," T.J. called, crossing his arms across the side of a memorial stone and resting his forehead between them. He began to count slowly, peeking underneath his arm to get a general idea of the direction they were going. It was only fair—the cemetery was way too big to not have a little advantage.

He finally reached one hundred and yelled as loudly as he dared, "Ready or not, here I come!"

With that he took off in the direction he had seen Matt go. He quickly looked from left to right behind the rows of stones as he ran as quietly as he could through the grass. He thought he saw some movement behind a tree.

"I've got you right where I want you," he said to himself smugly as he slowed to a tiptoe. He crept up to the tree, ready to pounce.

"Ha!" he called as he jumped around to the other side of the tree, only to find it unoccupied.

Not yet discouraged, he immediately turned around and took off on the search again. The moonlight should offer an advantage, he thought, as he scanned his surroundings with the keen eye of an experienced hide-and-go-seeker. He analyzed the trees and monuments around him, trying to determine where he might hide if he were on the other side.

Just southeast of him he spied a perfect place. It was a big white marble spire with a marble curb laid out in front of it to mark the plot. From his vantage point he couldn't see behind the curb, thus making it an ideal hiding spot. He chuckled to himself. He could imagine one of his poor unwitting buddies pressed to the ground on his stomach, head down, trying to breathe quietly, unaware of the fact that his hunter was about to close in for the kill.

T.J. skirted around to the right and kept low, ducking behind tombstones. If he snuck up well enough and off to the side of the grave, he could maybe avoid even having to chase his prey. He drew close.

Although he was training his eyes to the plot within the marble curb, he caught a flash of movement just behind the spire.

A grin passed over his face as he thought, "What a moron! How obvious can you get?"

He tiptoed over to the side of the spire, took a deep breath, and swung around the corner, crying "Gotcha!"

The look of expectant smugness was soon replaced with a furrowed brow of confusion.

"Oh, hey kid. Who are you?" he asked suspiciously.

The boy standing before him was small, brown-headed like him. He didn't look too much older than T.J. His skin was really pale and he had on funny clothes. What really startled T.J., though, was the blindfold he was wearing over his eyes.

"What's with the blindfold, man?" T.J. asked nervously, taking a few steps backward. There was no telling what kind of wackos hung out in cemeteries after dark.

The boy did not answer.

"Um, well, I'm T.J. I'm playing a game with my friends if you want to help," he said. "What's your name?"

The boy slowly reached behind his head and untied the blindfold. He slowly lifted it from his eyes and blinked. He squinted his eyes and blinked as if he had just stepped into brilliant sunshine. He looked perplexed as he gazed at his surroundings.

He tried to speak but first had to clear his throat.

"I'm David," he finally managed to croak hoarsely. "Have you seen my mother?"

T.J. regarded him guardedly.

"Nope, sorry pal," T.J. said, edging away from the strange boy. This "David" seemed kind of out of it and T.J. didn't feel like dealing with this character alone. As the boy turned his head, T.J. caught a glimpse of his neck in the moonlight. It was red and raw, like it had been chafed by something.

"Hey, are you alright?" T.J. asked nervously, never looking away from the angry red welts ringing the boy's small throat.

The boy nodded absently and turned away from T.J. Taking that as a cue to make his own exit, T.J. mumbled a "later," did an about-face, and began to jog off. He looked over his shoulder and saw the boy looking around on the ground around him confusedly, seeming to search for something in a slow and disoriented manner.

The strange encounter had taken the wind out of T.J.'s sails. Not caring about the game anymore, he looked around half-heartedly as he headed back to the starting point of the game. There he found most of his friends waiting for him impatiently.

"Where the heck have you been?" they called out to him as he trudged over to join his gang.

"We waited forever and you never showed," Adam said. "I thought maybe it was a trick, but then I got bored and came back and found these guys," he explained.

"More like you got scared," John said teasingly, punching Adam in the arm.

"I did find somebody," T.J. said quietly. He then related to them what had happened, how he had met this weird kid in a blindfold. He felt goose bumps pop up all over his body as he tried to describe the interaction with the kid. It didn't come off sounding as creepy as it had actually been, but the boys' interest was definitely piqued. They hadn't seen anything cool in the graveyard yet. Maybe if they found this weirdo the night wouldn't be a total loss.

T.J. led the pack back toward the monument where he had bumped into the kid named David. As they drew closer he could see the moonlight reflecting the white marble of the pillar.

"There it is," he said, and quickened his pace. Since he wasn't looking for anyone who was necessarily hiding from him, he approached the grave straight on.

As he drew up to the grave he stopped so abruptly that his friends bumped into him from behind.

He looked at the spire with a mixture of nausea and horror. Engraved on the front of it were the words, "Here lie the remains of David O. Dodd. Born in Lavaca County, Texas, Nov. 10, 1846, died Jan. 8, 1864." On the curb surrounding the plot where he thought his friends lay in wait was another inscription: "Boy Martyr of the Confederacy."

"Oh yeah, David O. Dodd," John said knowingly. His dad was a big Civil War buff and therefore he kind of was too. "My dad told me about him. When the Yankees were here during the Civil War they arrested this kid for being a spy for the Confederacy."

"Whoa, cool," his friends said. Espionage was exactly the kind of thing they were into.

Encouraged by their enthusiastic response, John continued.

"He was only, like, seventeen-years-old," he said. The boys looked at the dates and the graves, did some quick mental arithmetic and determined this to be true.

"They held him prisoner over at the Ten Mile House until he was found guilty. They hung him on a cold winter's day, after they blindfolded him with his own handkerchief. But they had messed up the gallows or something. Either the rope was too long or the platform too short, because it took him five minutes to die."

The boys paused and let this sink in. None of them noticed T.J., who looked white as a ghost and trembled with fear. He nearly passed out.

"He was finally strangled and they buried him here," John concluded, pleased for having remembered the story.

"Gosh, he wasn't much older than us," Adam remarked, awestruck by the story.

"Hey, T.J., where'd you say you saw that weird guy?" John asked him. "T.J.?"

T.J. said nothing but stood frozen on the spot. He stared so intently at the spire before him that his friends waved their hands in front of his eyes.

"Earth to T.J.," they said teasingly. They finally had to punch him on the arm to snap him out of whatever little spell he was in.

"Ow, cut it out," he said suddenly, rubbing the sore spot where they had pounded him on the arm. "Let's get out of here already. I'm ready to leave," he said and headed back toward the bike.

The other boys shrugged and straggled along behind him. As they trotted along they laughed and horsed around, but T.J. remained silent. He stared resolutely ahead of him as he led the boisterous boys back toward their bicycles. He knew that he had met the ghost of David O. Dodd. He trembled a little at the thought. The neck wounds, the blindfold, the funny clothes, it all added up. But if he tried to tell his friends he would never hear the end of it. There was no way would they believe him.

Over the next few years the boys matured, the desire for girls and parties and cars eventually replacing the desire to play hide-and-go-seek in a graveyard.

What his friends didn't know, however, was that T.J. became a regular visitor to Mount Holly Cemetery. He only had one destination in mind on his visits. He followed the same path he had followed that fateful night with his friends.

He went back because he had to know if what he had seen was real or just a hallucination. Although he never saw him again, he had to keep trying. He had to know if somewhere in Mount Holly Cemetery the strangled ghost of David O. Dodd, the Boy Hero of the Confederacy, still stumbled about moaning, "I'm David—have you seen my mother?"

The Weeping Widow of Chickamauga

The Weeping Widow of Chickamauga

Y'all lean a little closer together," the young father instructed. His wife and their two children squeezed a little tighter together, nestled between the wheel and the barrel of the cannon, shivering a little as they waited for him to focus. The young mother couldn't help but think that she had just about had enough touring for the day.

The flash nearly blinded them as Jim snapped the picture in the deepening twilight. It was mid-November at the Chickamauga Battlefield National Park, and the sun had already begun its steady descent to the west, and the wind seemed to blow a little chillier. When the family had started out on the seven mile self-guided car tour, the weather had been brisk yet pleasant, but the late autumn afternoon was beginning to feel more and more like early winter as their shadows grew longer.

"Alright, kids," Jim said, stowing his camera in his shoulder case and hiking it up on his shoulder, "y'all ready to head out?"

This questioned was greeted with an enthusiastic affirmative. They piled back into the maroon rental car and Sarah cranked up the heater. Jim grinned a little and let out a playful groan. This was always the way: he was perfectly comfortable but she was freezing. Now he had no choice but to roast a bit before Sarah finally chased the ice water from the veins in her feet.

While the kids argued over ownership of the Chickamauga picture book they had bought at the Visitor's Center, the couple assessed the time. The park closed at five, and though it was only four thirty and they hadn't completed their tour, they decided it was best to call it a day. The kids, though abnormally harmonious and well-behaved for most of the day, were beginning to tire a bit of the history tour. Plus, once they got hungry, some amazing transformations could occur in those kids.

The book they were squabbling over was full of pictures. Throughout the tour they had had fun trying to figure out which pictures lined up with which view they could see as they stopped along the tour. They had made plenty of pictures themselves too, straddling the barrels of cannons, leaning against the Wilder Brigade Monument, posing atop Snodgrass Hill. It didn't really dawn on the kids that the very places they were walking had seen the courageous fight and bitter death of eighteen thousand Confederates and sixteen thousand Union soldiers on two bloody September days in 1863.

The children had also learned from the book a little bit about the battle—as much as hyper kids on vacation could absorb anyway. They had learned that the Battle of Chickamauga had occurred during the Union offensive in Tennessee, the goal being to capture Chattanooga. This was considered in some ways to be a gateway to the Deep South, and the Union army wanted it bad. If they won it, it would be a decisive victory for the Union.

They also learned that although the Confederate army was the victor by the end of the battle (despite having lost more men in the bloody struggle), more fighting in Chattanooga proper a couple of months later finally determined the Union to be the conquerors of the strategically-located Tennessee city.

In the steadily deepening late-autumn evening, Jim carefully executed a three-point turn and headed back in the direction from which they had come. He reached over and grabbed his wife's hand. They exchanged a tired but contented smile, momentarily drowning out the still-squabbling kids in the back seat.

They had enjoyed exposing the kids to a little history that day, injecting something a little substantial into a trip that otherwise mostly revolved around pizza, go-carts, mini-golf, and amusement parks. Neither of them were what you might call a history buff, but they both had a lingering interest in history from their days in college.

As they continued their exit from the park, the bickering in the back seat began to rise in pitch a little.

"I had it first," Brandon said, snatching the book from the weaker hands of his little sister.

"Nu-uh, I did. Give it back! Moooom," Betsy countered in her best whiny voice, barely pausing in between her words.

Sarah rolled her eyes a little. This was becoming a pretty typical exchange, each kid playing their part like they had rehearsed it or something.

"Brandon, let your sister see the book for a few minutes," the mother said absently as she enjoyed the scenery. To have once been a site of such gore and bloodshed, it sure was beautiful land. Pastoral green grass, rolling hills, Tennessee forest: it really was a gorgeous place—over two hundred years and two months after the conflict anyway. If they had driven the same route then, the mangled bodies, disembodied limbs, blood-soaked grass, and screams of agony would have eclipsed the natural beauty that served as a backdrop.

Sarah's mild command went unheeded and the kids in the back continued their own conflict. It contiued to increase in volume, reaching a more fevered pitch.

"Brandon, really," she said glancing over her shoulder at him, "let your sister see the book for a few minutes."

"She already had it for, like, the whole tour," Brandon pleaded. It was always this way, he thought. Just because she was younger and whined her stupid head off she always got her way.

"Just do it," the mother said with a stern tone of finality as her husband guided the car down the tour road. Sarah scanned the horizon and saw lights beginning to flicker in the fields in the distance. Are those street lights, she wondered. It was way too late in the fall for fireflies to still be hanging around.

Sarah noted with satisfaction that the little spat in the back seat had subsided. Arguments sure do blow over quickly with kids, she thought.

She thought wrong. As she quizzically regarded the lights she saw flickering around the field, the struggle over the book geared up again. All of a sudden she heard a smack, the distinct sound of someone getting slapped. They usually let the kids try to fight their own battles, but they drew the line when a fight turned physical. That finally got Jim's attention as he turned angrily toward the backseat.

"If you kids don't knock it off, I'll—"

"Jim, look out!"

His wife grabbed his arm as he yelled and slammed on the brakes with both feet.

The car jerked to a stop and panting for breath, they both looked out the windshield at a figure in the road. The kids were finally silent too as they leaned between the front seats to get a better look.

The rental car had screeched to a halt just inches from what appeared to be a woman standing in the road. In the glow of their headlights they could make out a woman in a simple dress holding a flickering oil lantern standing just shy of their bumper.

Once he had caught his breath, the father rolled down his window and stuck out his head.

"I'm so sorry, ma'am," Jim said, "I swear I didn't see you standing there."

The woman looked distractedly at them and then stepped to the side of the road, examining the ground around her.

The couple exchanged a glance and a shrug as Jim pulled up the parking brake and stepped out of the car.

"Ma'am, are you alright?" the man asked. "I almost ran you over. I don't know how I didn't see your light."

The woman looked at the man backlit by the headlights of the idling car. Her blond hair was tucked back in a kind of net and he noticed when he looked down that her dress fell all the way to the ground. Tendrils of fog crept around the hem of her skirt.

"I am looking for my husband," the young woman finally said, her face glistening with tears. "I would not presume that you may have seen him?"

"Um, no ma'am, I sure haven't," Jim said hesitantly. He looked around the car and finally noticed what his wife had seen some minutes before: there were several flickering lights swinging around the field, stopping, stooping, then swinging again.

"I do not know how I shall ever find him in all this," the woman said desperately, looking around her with a sort of horrified disbelief.

"Well, it is a big park," the man agreed haltingly. "When was the last time you saw him?"

"Oh, many months have passed since last I saw him," the woman said, turning her head away. This struck the man as rather odd. He regarded her carefully, beginning to think that this woman was really out of it.

She looked around her and her hand flew to her mouth as she stifled a sob. "So many fell on this hallowed ground," she said, picking up her skirt and moving away.

"It's true," the man said. "Something like thirty-five

thousand or more, I think I heard. We just took a tour."

At that the woman looked at him with a confused expression, then slowly covered her eyes and began to weep. The kids pressed against the window and the mother craned her head.

"Jim?" Sarah called out questioningly. He waved his hand in a gesture of respectful dismissal and turned back toward the strange young woman.

"Thirty-five thousand! What a loss," she mumbled between sniffles, "what a tragedy. It is unthinkable!" He had to lean to hear her as she muffled her voice with a handkerchief, "I do not know how I might ever find Robert. I pray to God that I do not. I pray you too will not find your loved one in this desolate place," she said, gesturing toward his headlights.

"Oh, um, I'm not missing anyone. All present and accounted for I think," he said weakly, not sure what to say next in this rather odd conversation. He looked over his shoulder at the fog as it moved through the beams of his headlights.

The strange woman turned her back to him and began to shuffle away, her lantern swinging before her in the new darkness. She began to move toward a cluster of lights in the distance. Jim thought he could hear women sobbing and conferring intermittently, but he wasn't sure. Fog had begun to roll in so thickly now that it obscured the flickering lights around them, muting them almost to the point of extinguishing them from sight all together.

"I can give you a ride to the Center if you'd like. Maybe you can report your missing husband there," Jim offered.

She stopped and turned her head over her shoulder. "Thank you, sir, but I rode with my sister. I cannot leave until I know for certain that Robert is not on these fields."

He thought he heard a name called out from the direction the woman was heading.

"God grant me strength," he heard her say as she hurried off, disappearing into the thickening fog. The man continued to gaze where the strange woman had last stood. There was something odd and troubling about the exchange he had just had, but he couldn't put his finger on it. Maybe she was just crazy, maybe one of those history people that got a little too carried away, he rationalized.

"Jim?" his wife asked gently.

He continued to look over his shoulder as he turned his body back toward the car. He had one foot in when he swore he heard a cry of anguish coming from the fog. He gazed intently in the direction of the sound and froze as he concentrated on the sound. The cry of anguish began to meld with other strange moans and shrieks. He felt the hair on the back of his neck stand up as he strained his ears to the growing cacophony. The sounds began to wash over each other, peppered by moments of pregnant silence before breaking again into wails and weeping.

"Jim?" his wife asked again, questioningly but firmly this time. This snapped him out of his trance. When she had spoken the sound had stopped altogether, like someone flipping a switch. He hurriedly put his other foot in the car and shut the door. The exchange with the woman could have only lasted a few seconds, but it felt like he was entering a different world when he finally settled back into the car with his family.

"What was that all about?" Sarah asked.

Jim chuckled and shrugged. "Just some crazy lady, I guess."

"Her outfit looked funny," Betsy said from the back seat.

"She acted funny too," her father agreed, slowly easing back into normality. "I guess it takes all kinds," he said. "Now, who's ready for dinner?"

This question was once again greeted by an enthusiastic reply as he pulled up toward the park exit. Both he and his wife noticed that the book incident had been forgotten, thanks to the strange lady with the lantern.

As they pulled through the parking lot they saw an employee headed to her car. He figured he couldn't have a clear conscience if he didn't at least mention the eccentric lady he had seen wandering around the battlefield.

Jim rolled down his window and called out, "Excuse me, ma'am, but there's a lady wandering around out there. She said she's looking for her husband?" This last statement sounded more like a question than a statement.

The employee looked briefly in the direction of the field.

"Nothing to worry about, I'm sure," she said quickly with a tight little smile. "You folks have a pleasant evening."

Jim waved goodbye, rolled up the window, and headed toward the exit.

The employee got in her car and revved the engine. She sighed and shook her head. She knew what he had seen. No one ever really spoke of it, but her headlights and those of many others had also drawn the attention of some strange ladies wandering about the field. Here they wandered night after night, shining their lanterns about furtively but futilely. The doomed specters of these abandoned widows have been seen wandering the fields of Chickamauga forever in search of their fallen sweethearts. These many years later they still step carefully through the deformed bodies and discarded limbs lying in pools of fresh blood in the green September grass that only they can see, hoping they don't see a familiar face amidst the gore and carnage.

She knew it was a silly thought, but she hoped, deep down, that one day they might find what they were looking for. At least then they may know a little peace.

About the Author

Brice Camp lives and works in Alabama. She received her B.A. in English from the University of Alabama. She enjoys reading, writing, history, and Alabama football. She dedicates this book to her folks.